Winging It

Winging It

By

K C Carlton

Published by Mandrill Press www.mandrillpress.com

ISBN 978-0-9927320-6-6

Chapter 1
Author: James

We had visitors sometimes. One of my jobs was to welcome them at the gate and take them to the Master, and then show them around after he had talked to them, and sometimes they wanted to know why I wasn't dressed as a monk. The answer was as simple as it was obvious: because I wasn't one. I was a lay brother.

Monasteries were all over England at one time, before Henry VIII got rid of them, but that was long before the English colonies began and I suppose you could wonder why this one was in California. Don't. There are more things in California, Horatio, than are dreamed of in your philosophy.

I could see disappointment sometimes on the faces of the visitors. They'd have liked us to have green fields and cattle and sheep so that we could be self-sufficient and sell prime organic beef and make sheep's milk cheese the way the monks in Wensleydale did. A California monastery isn't like that. Wensleydale isn't Wensleydale any more, either; the milk comes from cows now and the cheese is actually made in Swaledale.

We did have chickens and they laid lovely eggs. We also had a market garden and a hectare of glass and we didn't go short of vegetables and salads. The tomatoes were a delight. Commercial growers give theirs lots of water because tomatoes are sold by weight and they want them to grow big and fat. If you want taste, let the toms go thirsty. Not enough to split the skins but enough to build up the concentration of salts in the fruit. The salts are what give a tomato its flavour.

We also had lots of fruit bushes, from which the monks distilled liqueurs that we sold at fancy prices. More money came in from a big print shop and a bakery that made more bread than we could eat ourselves and sold the rest along with the surplus from the garden. You should have tasted our Sourdough Rye.

When I went there in 1985 there were twenty-five monks and three lay brothers but mine was the first new face in fifteen years and, at forty-two, I was twenty years younger than the next youngest. There weren't any new recruits after me. Monks die just like any other old men and we were down to ten monks, with me as the only lay brother. The Master said he would keep the place going as long as he could. The land would sell for a lot of money and the Master said he would raise a mortgage and invest the money so that we could bring in paid help. I rang Bennie and told him to send the Master a million dollars without telling him who the money was from. That ended financial worries for a while and the workers were hired. I was The Gardener—Capital T, Capital G—but I had four people to help me and all four went home at night. It was the same in the bakery and the print shop; only the distillery was still reserved for monks alone. All of the help was male. We did allow women visitors, as long as they covered their heads and dressed modestly.

I went there so that I would be able to meditate and pray without the distractions the world outside the walls presented. I won't say I went there to find God because I was told a year or so before I arrived that you don't find God—He finds you—and my experience says that's right. His hand is always outstretched towards you; all you have to do is reach out and take it.

I ignored that outstretched hand for the first forty years of my life.

Chapter 2
Author: James & Lucy

Everyone has to start somewhere—I suppose that's obvious. For me, it was when I was eighteen. I had already spent two years in the Sixth Form—two because the school thought I could win a scholarship to Cambridge and in those days if you were at a state school you needed an extra year for that. It was the summer holidays and I was hitch-hiking around England with two friends. Three hitch-hikers is one too many for most lifts, so the way we worked it was, we'd separate each morning—two guys would go together and the other on his own. Next day, a different split. We were staying in youth hostels and we knew we might not all reach the same place on the same evening, so we had a list of the hostels we hoped to stay in for the next week. There were no mobile phones in those days.

The day I'm talking about, I was on my own. We'd left Shrewsbury Youth Hostel at nine in the morning and agreed to meet up again in Minehead. That was a long way and a big ask in the days before the M5 but we planned to spend three days exploring the Exmoor National Park so it didn't matter if we didn't all get there that night.

The guy on his own could usually get a lift more easily than the two together, so our rule was that he would wait just out of sight until the other two had been picked up. That particular day, it took a good hour before someone would stop for them which meant I wasn't standing by the road with my thumb out until after ten. People stopped for me but none of them was on a long journey; by three in the afternoon I'd only reached Hereford and it had taken five rides to get that far.

Then I got lucky. A man on his own in a Jaguar told me he was going to Bristol, which was about half way between Hereford and Minehead. Maybe I wouldn't get all the rest of the way that day, but there were hostels in Bristol, Cheddar and Street and with an early start next morning I was confident I'd knock off the distance between there and Exmoor fairly quickly. In any case,

Jaguars didn't stop often and I was not going to turn it down.

I was a shy youth but he was an educated man and he slowly drew me out. I told him where I was going and who with. I told him what I enjoyed at school and what I didn't. He asked whether I hoped to go to university and what I would study there—when I said I wanted to read history he said that that had been his subject, too, and he talked about English and European history in a way that did not make me feel small but did let me understand how much I had to learn. He said I looked in pretty good shape—did I play any sport? I told him I was in the local athletics club and did well at the longer distances like the mile; also that I loved cricket. What about rugby, he wanted to know, and I said I wasn't really big enough. Yes, he said, I was obviously fit but "you are quite slight, aren't you? You don't look eighteen—if I'd had to guess, I'd have said you were a year or two younger than that." Then he told me he'd been a flanker at school and university but he'd had to stop playing when he started work because he just hadn't had enough time. That was when I looked at him properly for the first time and I could see he had the build for a flanker—he must have been well over six feet tall and he had a big chest and broad shoulders but there wasn't much surplus fat on him. He'd called me "slight" and, compared with him, I undoubtedly was.

Then he asked about my family and I told him I had a father and a mother and a sister, and that my sister was four years older than me and would soon be leaving home to get married. He said that twenty-two was too young to marry, that he had married when he was too young and that that was why he was divorced. 'Well,' he said. 'One of the reasons.'

Then he asked me a question that left me speechless. Had I, he wanted to know, ever tried on my sister's knickers when no-one was looking? I was shocked into silence and I could feel that my face was bright red. He looked sideways at me and smiled. 'I thought so,' he said. 'Don't be embarrassed. Lots of boys do it if they have the chance.' He reached over and squeezed my thigh with his hand. Then he put his hand back on the wheel as though nothing had happened.

We passed through Ross-on-Wye and he started to talk about the history of the border between England and Wales over the centuries, but I wasn't fooled. He was thinking about me in a girl's knickers.

We stopped at a filling station. My chance to go came when he went into the kiosk to pay. I could take my rucksack, fade away and not come out again until he had driven off. I had the chance. I could do it. And I should do it, because he'd asked about wearing girls' underwear and he'd put his hand on my thigh and I knew those weren't normal things to do.

When he came back to the car and saw me still there, he smiled. It was a knowing smile. We drove off, but after five miles we came to a layby in which no-one else was parked. He stopped. Without haste, he put one hand on each side of my face, pulled my head towards him and kissed me on the lips.

I know what you're thinking. Why didn't I punch his lights out? Well, for two reasons. The first was that he was bigger than me, and very obviously stronger, and if a fight started it would be me who found himself being beaten up and not him. And the second…the second reason was that every single one of my buttons was pressed, lit up, switched on.

How had he known? What did he see in my face that told him? Yes, I had tried on my sister's knickers. I had wished so often that I was a girl. As a boy, and especially with a father like mine, I was expected to be driven, an alpha male, someone who imposed himself on the world. And I wasn't. What I dreamed of most of all was submission. To be able to lie down and say, "Take me." Girls were expected to submit. Boys were not. In the England of the time, it was that simple.

I had never had sex with anyone, male or female. At school, which like most secondary schools in those days was an all boys affair with a separate girls' school next door, we all talked about the intensity of our desire—for girls. And I had that. I did. But men weren't ruled out. I didn't really know what it was that men did together. I'd hear furtive, sniggering laughter in school about boys being "bummed" and didn't know what it meant to be "bummed." But I knew I'd like to find out.

And now here was this man talking to me about girls' underwear, touching my leg and kissing me on the lips.

It wasn't fear I felt; it was excitement. What possibilities might have opened up when I stepped, innocent and unaware, into his car?

When we were moving again, he put his hand on my thigh, right at the top. He kept it there most of the way to Bristol. I say kept it there, but actually it wandered a bit. Rubbed gently up and down. I could feel myself getting harder and harder. I moved my legs a little apart so that he could slide his hand all the way down and then bring it back up.

He said, 'Why don't you undo your buttons?' and I didn't stop to think; I just did it. It was like I was in some kind of daze, only half conscious of what I was doing and what he was doing.

With the flies undone, his hand was inside my jeans, on my underpants and then inside them. He rubbed gently, I got even harder than I had been before and the result was inevitable; I came all over the inside of my Y-Fronts. He patted my thigh. 'You're a sweetie,' he said.

We didn't say any more until we were on the outskirts of Bristol, when he said, 'I don't know where the youth hostel is. I can find out, if you want? Or you could come and stay the night at my place?'

Staying the night at his place was what I wanted more than anything in the world—except, maybe, staying more than one night at his place. 'Will there be anyone else there?'

'No. I live alone since my divorce. There'll just be me and you.'

'I'll come home with you, please. If you don't think I'll be too much trouble.'

'I think you'll be a delight. What's your name?'

'James.'

'James. You're not really a James, are you? Does your mother call you Jimmy?'

I licked my suddenly dry lips. 'She does,' I said. 'But, actually, my mother never wanted a boy. She wanted another girl. If I'd been a girl, she was going to call me Lucy.'

'Lucy. That's a nice name. You make an adorable Lucy. Could you be Lucy for me, do you think?'

My heart was pounding and I was sure I must be bright red. 'Yes,' I said. 'I can be Lucy.'

'I'm Ben.'

We stopped again, at a food store this time, and Ben told me to stay where I was while he got something for us to eat. He came out of the store with a full carrier bag and crossed the road to a branch of Marks & Spencer. (Marks only sold clothes in those days—they wouldn't be in the food business for several years). When he came back to the car he had another bag and he placed both on the back seat.

He had an imposing house off Clifton Down, near the river and the gorge. He told me to stay in the car while he opened the gate and then again as he unlocked the garage. After he'd driven in and closed the garage door, he said, 'Out you get, Lucy.' My heart thrilled when I heard myself addressed like that. I knew what my father would say if he saw me here in this state (I still hadn't buttoned up) and I simply didn't care. It felt like everything I'd wanted, everything I'd even dreamed of without daring or knowing enough to want it, was being given to me.

There was a washing machine in the garage. Ben looked down at the opening in the front of my jeans. 'That must feel a bit sticky. Why don't you take them off and I'll wash them? I took off my boots and jeans and then slipped off the Y-Fronts and dropped them into the washing machine he was holding open. He said, 'Why not get your other stuff out of your bag and wash those, too? If you've been travelling a week I'd guess you could do with some clean clothes.' So I did all of that, while he watched. When I was putting in the last pair of underpants I said, 'I'll have nothing to wear while these are washing.'

'I took care of that when I went to Marks & Spencer.'

'Oh.' Again that thrilling feeling as I wondered what he'd bought, what he wanted Lucy to wear.

There was a door from the garage into the house so it was possible to go in without first going outside again, and that's what we did. Ben was carrying the food bag and the Marks & Spencer bag and he put them both down so that he could take me in his arms. Apart from my socks, below the waist I was completely naked and standing up hard once more. As Ben kissed me, his hands drifted down my back and onto my bottom. That was a change I noticed in me; normally I'd have said "onto my arse" but now that I was Lucy I didn't have an arse; I had a bottom.

His tongue pressed forward and I opened my mouth to let it find my own. Kissing him—being kissed by him, because that was really what was happening—felt wonderful. I knew I would deny him nothing. His strong hands kneaded my bottom cheeks; I still didn't really know what he was going to do, but whatever it was I was going to let him.

One of his hands moved from the back to the front; he gently cradled me, then slowly stroked. 'You need a bath,' he said. 'You do know you're a bit smelly?'

'The showers in the last two hostels weren't too good. And I've done a lot of walking.'

By now we were in the bathroom. Ben turned on both taps and tested the water temperature with his hand. 'Undress,' he said. I did. When the bath was ready he stood up and kissed me again. I loved the way he held me close to him. I'd thought so often about how it would feel to be a girl, but now I realised that that wasn't really what I wanted—I could have all the good male bits and still be loved by a man as though I really were his Lucy.

The next bit was heaven because Ben didn't leave me to wash myself—he picked up the soap and did it for me. Every inch of me. He kept the best till last because, when everything else had been washed (and most of it had also been kissed) he told me to kneel in the bathtub and he did what he called "your lovely bits." First he soaped my bottom, running his hand up and down the crack and then inserting his fingers, slippery with soap—first one, then two, then three. All I could do at that stage was lean forward and hold on to the taps while his fingers worked deep inside me. I felt on the very edge of coming again—an edge I went over when one of his hands moved forward and petted and stroked till I could withhold my sperm no longer and I shot it into the air to spray down across the bath water.

Then he was holding a warmed towel, I was stepping out of the bath and into his arms and he was drying me. Once again, every inch of me; once again, with special attention to my "lovely bits."

'I'm going to have you,' he said. 'You can give yourself to me or I'll take you, but I'm going to have you. I have to.'

I lifted my face to be kissed again. 'Whatever you want,' I said, 'I want, too.'

'Anything?'

'Anything. I want to make you happy.'

'Have you ever done this before?'

'Never.'

'But you want it?'

'I want it.'

'It may hurt a little the first time.'

'I want it.'

Then he took me by the hand and led me into the bedroom.

It was a big bed, with fine cotton sheets. I had no idea where his money came from but it was clear that he had a lot of it and equally clear that he didn't mind using it to spoil himself with luxury. He drew back the top covers, took two pillows and laid them in the middle of the bed, one on top of the other. Then he laid me, face down, with my hips on the pillows and my bottom raised in the air. He said, 'Wait there.'

He went out of the room. When he came back, he showed me a pot of Vaseline. 'I'll do everything I can not to hurt you more than I have to.'

'I know you will.'

He took off his clothes. I peeked sideways; I wanted to see him. He was lovely. Longer and thicker than me, even though he was as yet only half erect. The feeling when his finger, covered in Vaseline, began to work its way into my tight little rosebud was indescribably beautiful and I became hard once more. Once again it was first one finger, then two, then three. He went back to the Vaseline three times to push more of it into me and I could feel from the easier way his fingers moved inside me how slick and slippery I was becoming. As he worked, I moved my legs further and further apart to give him room.

Then his fingers were gone. Once more I peeked, this time to see him covering his penis—I can't avoid that word any longer. It was by now fully hard and pointing upwards. He knelt between my outspread thighs. 'I want you to relax,' he said, 'as much as you possibly can. The more relaxed you are, the easier this will be and the less it will hurt.'

'I'll try.'

'And push back. While I'm pushing forward, push back.'

It did hurt, and I'm not going to pretend it didn't. It hurt. But not intolerably, and after he'd got the tip of himself into me it hurt a little less. He paused and then pushed again, gaining another inch or so and the hurt was less. He continued like that—take an inch, pause, take another inch—and at last his hips were resting against mine, and now it scarcely hurt at all and what pain there was didn't matter because I had what I wanted. A man completely inside me.

He stayed like that for a few moments and all I could think of, all I experienced, was the joy of giving myself. The joy of submission. I had wanted it and now I had it and so often when you finally get what you want you find it isn't what you'd hoped and that was simply and definitely not the case here. I was being loved and it was wonderful.

He kissed me on the cheek. 'Are you okay, Lucy? Do you want me to stop?'

'I'm fine,' I said. 'Do what you want to do. Whatever it is, I want it, too.'

And then, slowly at first but with increasing speed, he rode me. There is no other word I can think of that does it justice; he *rode* me. He slid in and out of me and at the end of each stroke, with every slap against my bottom, I let out a moan of ecstasy. He moved a hand to my hip, slid it beneath me and began to stroke me and now I was moving in time with him and I let out a cry as I spouted once more, this time into the pillows beneath me, and then he shouted, too, and I felt his sperm shooting into me and I was filled, with cock and with semen and with joy.

We lay like that for minutes that seemed like hours and then he lifted himself from me and slapped me gently across the bottom and kissed me on the back of the neck. I turned and hugged him to me, as tight as I could, and he wrapped his arms around me and hugged me back as he smothered my face with kisses. 'You are my wonderful Lucy,' he murmured. 'My beautiful, beautiful girl.'

When he got up, he again told me to stay where I was. He came back carrying the Marks & Spencer bag and started showing me things as he took them out. There wasn't a lot—pyjamas; three pairs of knickers; a t-shirt and a skirt—but what there was took my breath away.

The PJs were baby dolls, a top and panty set in soft cotton with a pattern of little pink flowers and a pink bow on each short sleeve. Two pairs of knickers were the full, navy blue cotton garment that girls in those days wore to school and they were particularly touching for me because they were the exact sort that I had several times extracted from my sister's drawer to try on while I had the house to myself; the third pair were loose white cotton. When I say loose, I mean that they were what I now know as French Knickers; the legs were not elasticated and did not hug the top of the wearer's thighs and I could imagine Ben, when he bought them, imagining sliding his hand up one of the legs. I say that because that is also what I imagined when I saw them, and I grew warm at the idea. The t-shirt was a t-shirt, and what can you say about those? (Except that it was pink and had the sweetest picture of a kitten on the front). And the skirt—I was almost delirious at the idea that I would not only be wearing knickers without worrying about my sister or my parents seeing; I'd be wearing a skirt over them.

Clearly, Ben had chosen these sizes based only on what he'd seen of me and I hoped so fervently that they would be a good fit. Equally clearly, these were not just to fulfil my fantasies—Ben had matching fantasies of his own. I wanted to be Lucy for him; he wanted the same thing.

Ben took some sheets from a box of man-size tissues. 'Look, Lucy, let's be sensible here. You're going to be leaking for a little while and you won't want to spoil your new knickers as soon as you have them on. Let's make a little pad out of tissues to absorb the leaks until they stop. Now. Which pair do you want to wear first?'

I picked up one of the navy schoolgirl pairs. 'I'll save the lovely loose-legged ones till tomorrow.'

He folded the tissues into the pad he had suggested and told me to hold it in place against my bottom while he pulled the knickers over my feet and up my legs. 'Tomorrow? Don't you have to be on your way in the morning?'

'I do if you want me to be. I don't actually *have* to be in Minehead till the day after, so I could stay another day. If you wanted me to?'

He put his arms round me and hugged me tight. 'Oh, sweetheart. That would be wonderful. Another day! And another night?'

'And another night,' I affirmed as I pulled up the waist so that the knickers were snug around my bottom.

He kissed me so passionately I was almost afraid I might suffocate. Then he broke off to hold the skirt over my head and drop it to my waist. 'It fits really well,' he said.

'It does, doesn't it.' I looked at myself in the mirror to see it hang half way down my thighs. I picked up the t-shirt and wriggled into it. 'I'm sorry I don't have breasts.'

He kissed me again. 'Don't you dare apologise. For anything. You have everything I could possibly want. You *are* everything I want.' He stood back to look at me, then took me by the hand. 'Come and sit in the kitchen while I make dinner.'

Chapter 3
Author: James & Lucy

He looked serious as he prepared the meal. 'You do realise what a risk I've taken, Lucy?'

I did realise. What we had done was against the law. The Sexual Offences Act would not be passed for another five years and, even when it was, homosexual acts would only be lawful if performed in private by consenting men who were at least twenty-one years of age. I was eighteen. He would be accused of seducing a minor and he would go to jail. He had taken a hell of a risk in giving in to temptation.

'You can trust me,' I said.

'I know I can, Luce. I've behaved myself for so long, but when I saw you I just knew you had the same desires as me and I knew you were a decent person.'

The word "gay" was not in common use then; the world would call us queers if they knew. It was not a good time to be the way we were.

He said, 'How did you feel while we were in bed together?'

'The same way I feel now. As if I'd finally accepted myself as what I am. I feel fulfilled. For the first time in my life.'

He poured two glasses of wine. People in Britain didn't drink wine at that time. I'd never seen my parents touch a drop. It was lovely.

Ben said, 'Do you always sit with your legs crossed?'

'I never do.'

'You're doing it now, my sweet. It's a real girly thing to do.'

And I was. What I had said was true; I never crossed my legs at home. But then, I never wore a skirt and knickers at home. My sister sat like this, my mother sat like this and, now that I was dressed as a girl, I sat like this, too.

Ben put the dinner on the table and topped up both of our glasses. He could cook, I'll say that. The meal was better than anything I'd ever had at home. The wine helped, too.

When we had finished eating, he loaded the dishes into

the dishwasher. We didn't have one of those at home—not many people in Britain did at that time. Then he turned to me. 'Why don't you stand up, darling, and let me check whether you're still leaking? That's right. Just lift up your skirt for me.' So I did, and he rolled the knickers gently to my knees and removed the little pad of tissues. He rolled the knickers completely off before standing to throw the stained tissues into the waste bin. Then he took my hand once again and this time he took me into the sitting room. This room was huge, with two big sofas and a number of chairs. He led me to one of the sofas and eased me into it, holding my skirt up by the hem so that I wasn't sitting on any part of it. 'I'm going to teach you how to suck,' he said.

He turned me sideways and lay me down on my back. Sitting by my feet, he raised the skirt again, laying it over my tummy. (And once again I found myself in a girly world, because I would never normally have used the word "tummy"). He placed one hand on me and smiled to see how aroused I already was. His fingertips grazed my sack, stroked softly and then went down to the place between sack and bottom. Without conscious thought I separated my legs. A moan slipped from my lips; I simply couldn't help it. He was in control of my body and I was not. While that hand made continuous circular motions on the unbelievably sensitive place, the other took me between thumb and forefinger. He kissed it, then took the tip into his mouth. Now his mouth began to move slowly, rhythmically, up and down the length of my penis. Drawing it in and letting it out. Drawing it in and letting it out. I had never felt excitement like this and the end was coming fast. I said, 'I'm going to come.'

'Mhm.'

'But I'm going to come *now*.'

He took his mouth away but kept his face very close. His hands continued their separate, rhythmic play. And then it was on me in a frenzied rush; I was throbbing and the juice was flooding out of me and spattering all over his hands and my stomach.

I lay back in disbelief. Ben raised himself above me and

smiled. 'Thank you for the warning, angel.'

'I was scared of doing it in your mouth.'

'You were right not to want to do that. Now clean yourself up, get dressed and let's talk.'

So I went into the bathroom to wipe myself with a flannel soaked in warm water, and then into the kitchen to retrieve my knickers. I put them on and smoothed down my skirt. Then we sat on the sofa, side by side. Ben put his arm round my shoulder and I snuggled into his side. He put his hand under my chin, turned my face up to his and kissed me.

'You took a chance, too, Lucy.'

'Me?'

'You. I want you to promise me you'll be more careful in future.'

'What do you mean?'

'There are lots of queers out there who would have taken advantage of you and hurt you. Some of them would have killed you afterwards to stop you talking.'

I shuddered. 'How do I know which is which?'

'You don't. Not in advance. So promise me.'

'I promise.'

'I gave you a chance to walk away. When I stopped at the filling station I didn't need petrol. I went into the kiosk so that you could go if you wanted to. I was pleased you stayed, but I didn't force you. Some men would have stayed in the car and locked the door and not let you out until they'd had what they wanted. Whether you wanted it or not.'

It must have been obvious that I was shocked.

'You're sexually active now, Lucy. You've discovered who you are and you've found out how much you like having sex with a man. You'll want to have more. And I won't be there to protect you.'

That silenced me for a while. What had happened—what *was* happening—between me and Ben seemed so loving, so full of sweet affection, that it made me sad to think that there were men, other men, who would see it as an opportunity to hurt. At last I said, 'So what do I have to do?'

He kissed me again. 'Don't be so trusting. Men who like men will know what you are. Just like I did. And they'll want you—just like I did. If you give in as quickly with them as you did with me, you'll often be all right. And sometimes you won't. It only takes one bad one, Luce.'

We sat quietly while I digested what he had said. After a while he got up, went into the kitchen and made coffee. He brought it in in a tray. 'I was so excited at the idea of blowing you, I missed out on this stage.'

On the tray, as well as the coffee pot, cups and cream jug, were a bottle of whisky, a small jug of water and two glasses. He poured coffee for us both and handed my cup to me. Then he poured the whisky, a lot into one glass and less into the other, and handed the smaller one to me. 'I'm guessing you haven't drunk whisky before?'

I shook my head. 'You're right. I mean, I haven't.' Eighteen year olds reading this now will probably laugh, but eighteen today is not like eighteen then.

'This is the Macallan. A straight malt. You don't add ice and you don't add ginger ale. I think in yours, though, a little water might be a good idea.' He poured some into the glass I was holding.

We drank Nescafé at home, and the coffee Ben had made was better than anything I had ever tasted. The whisky was something else. It was like being cuddled by a strong man. I felt warmth in the pit of my stomach. Ben put his hand on my thigh, pushing the skirt up out of the way so that he could gently stroke the bare flesh. 'How do you feel?'

I turned towards him, smiled, lifted my face so that I could kiss him on the cheek. 'I'm floating. Happier than I've ever been in my life.'

'Happier?'

'More content. Like I belong here. With you.'

'This swallowing thing is something else you need to be

aware of. Most queer men do what we just did. They'll use their mouths to bring you to the point, but they don't want you to come in their mouths and you won't want them to come in yours. Making you swallow isn't about affection, it's about dominance. A man who wants to come in your mouth is a man who wants to humiliate you. Remember that. Women swallow, or so I believe, but men don't.'

I rested my head on his shoulder, only moving it to take a sip of coffee or whisky. We stayed like that for a long time. Then Ben said, 'Why don't you go and get ready for bed, sweetheart?'

The PJs had slipped out of my mind; they came back now. I went into the bedroom and undressed. I put on the cotton panties and snugged them around my bottom, and then I slipped the top over my head. I stood in front of the mirror, turning this way and that. Ben had said I made an adorable Lucy and adorable was exactly how I felt I looked now. I felt very shy as I came downstairs and stepped into the sitting room. 'What do you think?'

'Oh. Oh, Lucy. You look wonderful. Come here.' He patted the sofa beside him. As I sat down, he said, 'You look sad.'

'I am, a little.'

'Why?'

'Oh…because I'm not the girl I should be. I'm dressed like a girl, but I'm not one.'

'Lucy.' He was very stern. He placed his hand on the front of the panties, where my penis stood up rock hard. 'If you were a girl, you wouldn't have one of these, to pleasure me with. And if you were a girl, I wouldn't have brought you here.'

'I know. I'm just being silly.'

'Come on,' he said, standing up. 'There's only one place for us now and that's bed. You go and get into it while I lock up down here.'

* * *

Lying between those lovely sheets waiting for him, I let my mind run over everything that had happened during that day—a day that I knew had changed my life. My first ride in a Jag. His question about wearing my sister's underwear. His hand on my thigh. His kiss. The way he had stroked me inside my pants, bringing me to my climax. How it felt to have him inside me. The lovely things he had bought me. Being sucked to another climax. And now…what new things was I about to experience, to learn?

I heard Ben in the bathroom and then he came to where I was. 'I've put your things in the dryer,' he said. 'They'll be ready to go when you are.'

I felt a sudden pang as I realised that this heaven could not last for ever, but I knew he was right—it couldn't. I had to rejoin that other world, pretending once more to be what I was not.

I watched as he took off all of his clothes. By the time he was down to his underpants I could see again what a big, powerful man he was. Big and powerful and yet gentle and loving towards me. He didn't seem to have any pyjamas of his own because he stripped off the underpants and got into bed naked just as he was.

He sat and looked at me and I revelled in the approval in his gaze. He put a hand under my top and began to rub my tummy and my chest. He leaned forward and kissed me. And then I remembered what he had said earlier: that he was going to teach me how to suck. Teach *me*. He had taught by showing. The conclusion was obvious.

'Lie down,' I said. He did so without hesitation. I knelt beside him. I held him. He pulsed in my hand. I leant forward and kissed the tip. As I did so, I realised what he'd been doing in the bathroom; he had been washing himself in preparation for this. So that he would be clean and sweet smelling for me. And sweet tasting? I felt so touched to know that he would be so thoughtful.

Whatever dreams I had had, I had never dreamed of doing this. I would have said that it was a dirty thing and one that I did not want to do. The moment I took his hot tip into my mouth, I knew that I would have been wrong.

I wrapped my tongue around it. He let out a little moan and I was filled with pride that I could have this effect on such a man. I began to copy what he had done to me, letting my mouth slide up and down the shaft, all the time running my tongue around it. He had kept his teeth away from mine, and I did the same for him. I cupped his balls in one hand, letting the tips of my fingers play gently on that sensitive place he had shown me between balls and bottom, and with the other I stroked whatever part of him was not at that moment in my mouth. His moans were coming more frequently now and his hands came down to wrap themselves in my hair. 'You should grow this longer,' he said.

I took my mouth away long enough to say, 'My father would have a fit,' and then returned to what I had been doing. 'Oh, Luce,' he gasped. 'Oh, Lucy. Oh, my darling.' And then his hands moved my head very firmly away, his back arched from the bed and he came, splashing my hands and his stomach in equal measure.

When he was done I put my mouth back where it had been and licked him clean, all the way up to the tip. His sperm was warm and salty. I sat back on my heels. I smiled.

He opened his eyes, which had been closed during his final tremors. He held out his arms and I sank into them.

'How do you feel?' he asked.

'Complete. I am a proud girl who has brought her man to satisfaction. I think. You *are* satisfied?'

He laughed. 'As rarely in my life before. You were born for this, my darling. Lie down beside me.'

I did so and he pulled the blanket over us, wrapping us both together in a warm cocoon of love. He said, 'Turn your back to me,' and when I did so he pulled me close, pressing my back against his front and pushing his legs forward so that I was lying in a seating position, if that makes sense, and his legs were the chair on which I sat. He kissed my back. Gently, he stroked my tummy. I fell asleep.

It was two in the morning when I woke, Ben was asleep and we were in the same position as we had been when I fell asleep except that his hand was inside my panties. I got up to go to the bathroom. When I came back, he was awake. I got back into bed in the same position as before and he kissed me on the back of my neck and put his hand on my hip. I took hold of it and put it back inside my panties. I fell asleep again.

I was woken about five hours later when Ben went to the bathroom in his turn. When he came back to bed, I lay on my back and held my arms up to him. He came into them and we hugged. He lifted my top and began to rub my chest gently, kissing me all the while. From time to time his thumb would rub gently against my nipple. I notice that I keep saying "gently"; gentleness was the heart and soul of what he was doing. He brought his mouth down to the other nipple and played with it, licking, kissing, sucking and blowing. I had never realised that my nipples were capable of standing up, but they were and they did.

The hand went lower, rubbing my tummy now instead of my chest. I was very aroused; when I put my hand on him I discovered that he was, too. He broke off for a moment to pick up a bottle from his bedside table. It had a press button on top and he took my hand, sprayed something that felt like a thin oil into my hand and then returned my hand to where it had been. As I stroked him I could feel him getting harder.

He took my waistband in both hands and I lifted my bottom to let him roll the panties down. When they were around my ankles I shuffled my feet to kick them off. He put his hands on the inside of my knees and I willingly moved my legs apart. He threw back the blanket, rolled between my legs, hooked his hands under my knees and lifted them. I still didn't really know what to do, so he put my hands under my knees. 'Can you hold your legs up like that?'

I kissed him. 'Of course I can.'

'Do you want this?'

'Of course I want it.'

'We'll be making love looking at each other.'

'Good.'

He took his little pot of Vaseline and began to rub it tenderly into my bottom. 'I'd better get some more of this.' When he had enough in me, he spread it over his hard cock. Then he placed himself at my waiting entrance.

It was easier than the day before, but still he was patient, going slowly, advancing a little at a time and rubbing my chest, my tummy, my nipples while he was sliding into me. At last he was all the way in. He paused as he had done yesterday, but this time he was able to kiss my face, my shoulders, my neck and my lips while he waited. All of his weight was supported on his elbows, but that didn't stop the stroking and nor did it prevent him from grabbing his bottle of oil and spraying some on his hand, as he had on mine. And now I saw the point of the oil because, as he began to slide in and out of me, he wrapped the hand with the oil on it around my cock and began to work it with his hand—up, round, down, from time to time gently touching the tip. I had done this to myself, many times, though without the oil, but the sensations I was feeling now were better than anything I had known before.

He said, 'You don't need to hold your legs any more,' so I let go of them and wrapped my arms around his neck and my legs around his back and he fucked me. I haven't used a word as strong as that before (though I shall, again and again as my life's story unfolds) but that's what he did. He fucked me. And I loved it.

And then I came, in his hand, splashing warm seed all over my tummy. And then he came, in my bottom. And we subsided onto each other, fulfilled and spent.

After we had lain entwined for a little while, Ben turned me onto my front. 'Stay like that,' he said as he padded off. He came back with a soft towel, warm from the bathroom rail, and a flannel that he had soaked in warm water and wrung out. He cleaned and wiped my bottom with the flannel and dried me with the towel. Then he got back into bed, pulled the blanket over us once more and turned me onto my side so that we could cuddle.

We didn't get up till nearly nine, which seemed awfully late to me. It was a weekday and I knew that my father would have left the house more than an hour ago. I said, 'Don't you have to go to work?'

'Not if I'd rather spend the day with you. Which I would.'

'Oh. Won't anyone mind?'

'If they do they'll have the good sense to keep quiet about it. I own three businesses, Lucy. We make stuff, things for the hotel business, and we sell all over the world. None of them knows I'm not visiting one of the others today, or seeing a customer. I'll call my secretary about ten o'clock and tell her I'm taking the day off.'

So now I knew where the money came from.

'Scrambled eggs?'

I nodded. 'That would be lovely.'

'Some bacon with it?'

'My mother would say you're spoiling me.'

'You're worth it. What knickers have you got on?'

'These.' I lifted my skirt so that he could see the white cotton pair with the loose legs.

He lifted my chin and kissed me. 'That's something to look forward to.'

There was a patio outside, with chairs, a table and a sun umbrella, and after breakfast we went and sat on it. We were far enough away from the neighbours, and the hedge was high enough, that we didn't need to worry about being overlooked. Ben took my hand in his. 'Tell me how you're feeling?'

I started to tell him again what I'd told him yesterday; about the proud girl who had brought her man to satisfaction. He stopped me. 'You're not a girl. You're a young man. A young queer man. Don't, Lucy—I see you starting to pout and I don't want you to do that. You have a cock, Luce, a beautiful cock that gives us both pleasure, and girls don't have those. And I'll say it again: if you were a girl you wouldn't be here with me. Would you rather not be here with me?'

'No,' I whispered.

'Look, Luce, it isn't a crime to be queer. Well, it is, but only to the idiots who make the laws. It isn't a crime against nature. Lots of animals mate with their own sex and nobody wants to lock them up. That's good, you're smiling. Some men, most men probably, only ever think of mating with a woman. And then there are the lucky ones like you and me who prefer the real thing.'

Now I really was smiling. I'd been about to cry when he— this man who had bought me girls' clothes and treated me so much the way I wanted to be treated—had told me I wasn't a girl and now I was laughing.

'Your mother wanted a girl and not a boy and she let you know that. You love your mother and probably when you were a little boy your subconscious wanted to make her happy by giving her what she wanted. Your father wanted somebody a bit bigger, a bit more aggressive, a bit more like the standard male model and you recoiled from that. It could have gone the other way, Lucy. Deep down where the real decisions are made which is a place we never go to and aren't really aware of, you could have decided to be all man. You didn't. There's a lot of the feminine in you, Lucy, and I love that.

'It doesn't make you a girl, though.'

'No,' I said, still so quietly the word could scarcely be heard.

'Queers put themselves into categories. They call themselves dom and sub, for dominant and submissive. You know which you want to be, don't you?'

I nodded. 'A sub.'

'Some say they're a top or a bottom instead. It's the same thing. Do you understand?'

I did. I didn't want to, but I understood. I raised the hem of the skirt in my hands. He would have been able to see my knickers beneath. 'What about these?'

'That's play, Luce. Good sex has lots of playing in it. You

like pretending to be a girl who's submitting. I like having someone who's pretending to be a girl pretending to submit. When we dress you up, the play seems more real. And you get pleasure out of wearing those things, and who would deny you that? And I get pleasure out of seeing you do it.' He leaned over and hugged me. 'Especially when you look so sweet in your girl's clothes. Where are you planning to go to university?'

The sudden change of subject startled me. 'Cambridge. If I get the A Level results I'm supposed to get.'

'That has to be first choice. Obviously. Why don't you apply for Bristol as well? As a back-up?'

'I never thought of it.'

'If you get into Bristol you could come and live here. As my lodger. If you needed it to get your full grant I'd give you a receipt for rent but I wouldn't take any money from you so you'd be better off than the other students. And I'd feed you.'

'What would your neighbours think?'

'I'd tell people you were my nephew. When we met people you could call me Uncle. You'd have your own bedroom for the look of the thing when you brought students back here.'

'But I'd sleep with you?'

'Oh, I do hope so, Luce. Look, it's twelve months away. You don't need to decide now.'

But I had decided. 'I'll apply to Bristol. If I don't make it to Cambridge, I'll be here.'

'Take my address when you leave tomorrow. If you get in to Bristol, send me a card with your address on and sign it Lucy. I'll write to you, a nice formal letter to show your parents saying this house is on the university digs list and we've been assigned to be your lodging during your time here.'

'We?'

'I'll pretend to have a wife. Your parents might smell a rat otherwise.'

* * *

That evening after dinner, Ben said, 'You remember what I said about sex and play?'

'Yes?'

'Well. How would you like to play out a little fantasy?'

'I'd love to.'

'Okay. Here's the story. You are Lucy. I'm your guardian. You've been a naughty girl and I have decided you need to be punished. You okay with that?'

A little shiver went through me. 'Yes. I am.'

'Right. Stand there,' and he pointed to a point about two feet from a chair that was a little higher than the others in the room. 'I'll go and get what I need.'

When he came back into the room he was holding the bottle of oil, the jar of Vaseline, a towel and a table tennis bat. He sat in the chair in front of which I was standing. 'You've been very naughty, Lucy.'

'I'm sorry.'

'Do you mean, "I'm sorry, sir?"'

'I'm sorry, sir.'

'Sorry doesn't cover it, Lucy. You have to be punished.'

I put my hands over my face. The little shivers now were running riot. 'Please don't hurt me, sir.'

'I don't want to hurt you, Lucy. But I'm afraid I don't believe you will learn your lesson without corporal punishment. Take off your skirt.'

'Oh, sir! No! *Please.*'

'Don't make me have to tell you again, my girl. Take off your skirt.'

With a great show of hesitation, I undid the top button of the row down the front of the skirt. Then I undid the second button. Then I let the skirt fall to the floor around my ankles. I know it was all staged, but it felt so real. I felt myself blushing bright red.

'Don't leave it there, girl. You have to be more careful with your clothes than that.'

'Yes, sir. I'm sorry, sir.' I picked up the skirt, folded it carefully and placed it over an armchair.

'Now your t-shirt.'

'Oh, but *sir*. I'll have almost nothing on.'

'Lucy!'

'Yes, sir.' And I removed the t-shirt, folded it and placed it on top of the skirt. All I had on now was the loose-legged knickers.

'That's better. Now come and stand here beside me.'

I did. He laid the towel in his lap. He took my hands in his and pulled me forward so that I lay face down across his knees. And then it happened, this thing that I had dreamed of when first I saw these knickers. One big hand pressed on the small of my back, holding me down. The other stroked my thigh, then slid up, toyed for a moment with the hem and slipped inside to smooth the skin of my bottom. 'You have a beautiful arse, Lucy,' he said. 'You have an arse that would tempt the straightest man.'

His finger ran up the cleft between my buttocks and down again. The hand was withdrawn. He took the waistband in both hands and drew it down to my knees. One hand went back to holding me in place. There was a pause. And then I yelped as the other hand descended with a stinging crash onto my upraised bottom.

Another pause, another smack, another yelp.

It went on. I felt my bottom becoming warm under the constant barrage that varied only in the place he chose to deliver his smacks. My cock was hard, straining for release.

At last it was over. He picked up the table tennis bat and held it under my nose. 'Shall I continue with this, Lucy?'

'Oh, please sir, no. I've learned my lesson. I promise.'

'Very well. Let that be enough for today.' He put down the bat and picked up the oil. He sprayed some onto my bottom and began to rub it gently into the hot, bruised flesh, soothing the pain.

It was too much. My cock jerked and I came into the towel.

Ben was not done yet. He dipped a finger into the Vaseline and then into the space between my bottom cheeks, pushing into the welcoming rosebud. I spread my legs as far as I could. The greased finger worked me as a potter moulds clay. I felt at ease; held; cared for; content.

He desisted. 'Stand up, girl.'

I stood. Ben stood, too. He put one hand on each side of my face, drew me forward, kissed me. 'Kneel,' he said. 'On your knees and on your elbows. Present yourself for mating like a bitch to a dog.' I did so. Ben stripped off his clothes.

And then, for the third time in twenty-four hours, I was filled. With cock. With sperm. With happiness. With love.

Chapter 4
Author: James's Sister

Time to introduce myself and explain what this book is and why it's available for you to read.

Jimmy Carlton was my brother. When he died two years ago, at what these days is the young age of sixty-eight, he left everything to me. For all the partners he'd had throughout his life, male and female, there was no-one else to leave it to. I was very happy to receive his bequest; Jimmy was a rich man and his money will make the last years very comfortable for my husband and me and our children will welcome what's left.

One gift, though, I'm less certain about.

Jimmy knew he was dying; when I visited him in the nursing home a week before the end he gave me his laptop. 'Don't turn it on till I'm gone,' he said. 'But don't delay after that.'

The hard disk on Jimmy's laptop was almost empty, and I took that as his way of telling me that the three folders remaining were important and I had better read them. Everything else had been wiped clean.

Folder Number One contained a single file with instructions on where he wanted to be buried and how he'd like his death to be celebrated. The instructions involved lots of champagne and I was happy to comply.

Folder Number Two told me where all his assets were and how to make sure I got my hands on them; it also listed people he owed money to and asked me to make sure they were paid.

And the third folder was this book, together with some short stories and more than a hundred photographs.

I dealt with the first folder in days and the second in weeks. I've spent two years agonising over the third.

Why did Jimmy write this story of his life, and why did he leave it to me? What did he want me to do with it? I didn't know the answers to those questions and I still don't. Was it just for me, or did he want me to publish it? Did he simply want me to know about the shocking things he'd done in his life? Was it even true? And if the answer to that question was Yes, was it completely true or just a little bit true? Autobiography or a novel? Faction or fiction? The photographs suggested that there was more fact than fiction.

I needed answers to these questions before I decided what to do with the book. My first thought was to hire a private investigator—he'd left more than enough money for that—but the more I thought about it, the less I liked the idea. A private eye looks for evidence of crime, whereas what I wanted was fact and journalists are the experts at that. So, I talked to a retired newspaper man who would have known some of the people Jimmy talks about. I offered him a fee of a quarter of a million pounds plus all his expenses, which I knew would be considerable, to investigate Jimmy's story. In return for the fee he signed a non-disclosure agreement and assigned to me copyright in everything he wrote on the subject.

The investigative journalist—I'm going to call him IJ—kept me informed of everyone he talked to and everything he learned. Three weeks ago, he sent me his final report. This is an extract, and I'd like you to keep what he says in mind while you're reading the rest of this book:

The overall conclusion is that your brother's book is
autobiography and not fiction; it is, essentially, his version
of what actually happened. His truth, if you like. But
journalists learn to be sceptical around that word, "truth."
One person's account of what happened may not tally with
the story as told by someone else who was there. Neither
of them is—necessarily—lying; people see events and
motivations differently.
Many people were, initially, reluctant to talk to me but I
could usually overcome their resistance by telling them
that James's narrative existed, that it was backed up by
photographs and that the person who had the narrative and

*photographs was considering making them public. When
they knew that, most witnesses became eager to put their
own version—their own narrative, if you like. It usually
confirmed what James had said, but offered a different slant.
And, sometimes, I was presented with a version of events
(or, more usually, motivations) that differed completely from
the one you have.*

*To take one example: Ben. In Chapter Seven of your
narrative [James's Sister's Note: This is now Chapter Ten
because of the additional material I have incorporated]
James gives a précis of a series of conversations in which
Ben describes the loss of a lover in tragic circumstances
and says that he had gone twelve years without a man since
then. This was the story he told James and the last part of it
is simply not true. Ben was no stranger to the picking up of
hitchhiking young men and boys. Often—usually—he had
to accept that what had looked, standing by the road, like a
hot prospect was not; that the risk was too great, but he had
been lucky often enough to keep looking. That was what he
had been doing when he drove through Hereford—looking
for a lucky strike. When he saw James with his rucksack
on the ground beside him and his thumb extended, he saw
enough to make the investment of a little time worthwhile.
Much later, when Ben and James were an established item,
Ben would tell James his story. It would culminate in the
death that had never actually happened of a young man who
thought of himself as a girl and dressed like one but who
had never actually existed followed by years of grieving
chastity that Ben had never actually practised. Ben was
good at inventing stories to appeal to the particular young
man in his company.*

*Something else I can say about Ben is that he described
himself as divorced and in fact he'd never been married. I
don't know whether James ever found that out, but it's one
more lie told by Ben when he was reeling James in.*

Ben was more than twenty years older than James and he's been dead for some time, but the man who told me this saw nothing wrong in what Ben did. In this man's view—well, I'll tell you what he said:

"Sex between men and boys—and in England in 1959 you were a boy at eighteen and not yet a man—is right. It's what nature intended. The Greeks knew that, three thousand years ago. Fornication between men and women is necessary for the human race to continue but that is not where pleasure lies. Society in 1959 did not see things that way and so you had to dissemble. Ben was good at dissembling. To some people lying might have been a more accurate word, but Ben knew better than that. He knew that if he had stopped his Jaguar and said, 'Come with me; I want to go to bed with you," there was very little chance that James would get into his car. But going to bed with James was exactly what Ben hoped to do if things turned out as he wanted. And James would enjoy it, and would learn the truth about himself and about male to male sex. Showing someone the one true way to pleasure is a good thing, isn't it? And worth a little dissembling?"

When you read that, I think it's worth bearing in mind that this is the defence paedophiles use. "It's what s/he wanted." "I did it out of love." "The Ancient Greeks did it." The book suggests that your brother saw Ben as an affectionate and thoughtful lover; it's as well to remember that he was, in fact, a sexual predator.

There is a lot more in IJ's report and I'll reproduce some of it in the course of this book. For now, I think this is also worth keeping in mind:

It's your brother I'm talking about and I know you regarded him highly. (Actually, after reading what he left behind and talking to people who knew him, I regard him highly, too). But I don't think we'll get far in understanding him unless we accept that James was a sexual being—with women as well as men. When he talks about having had an intense sexual desire for men, he is telling only half the story. As one person who knew him well said, "Jimmy would fuck a

34

snake if it had armpits."

*By the way, if you do decide to publish your brother's story,
I strongly recommend that you change most of the names.
Some of these people are well known, some of them have
powerful friends with a lot to hide and being sued for libel
might be the least painful thing you face. And you'd be wise
to keep those photographs to yourself.*

I've spent the last three weeks thinking about IJ's final report and
I've decided that Jimmy left his book to me because he wanted
it to be published—so here it is. In many ways it's a historical
document, tracing as it does the activities of homosexual men in
England from a time when all male homosexual activity was illegal
to one where we might sometimes wish it was still the love that
dare not speak its name. I've taken IJ's advice; the names have been
changed (starting with Ben's); the photographs are in a very secure
place; and even some of the films Jimmy appeared in are called
here by invented names.

Before we move on, let me say something about my
brother. At the time this story begins, Jimmy was eighteen (though
Ben was right—he looked younger) and he was beautiful. No other
word does him justice. A shade over five feet ten, slim but nicely
muscled from all the exercise he took, wavy brown hair, blue eyes,
a complete lack of the acne that disfigures so many boys of his
age. All the girls in our street watched him as he went by, and so did
their mothers. It never occurred to us that men might be watching
him, too—looking back, those seem very innocent days.

He didn't know that he was beautiful—our parents didn't
believe in letting their children get above themselves, by which I
suppose they meant conceited—and there was a shyness about
him that stopped him talking to those girls who watched him. If
he had, he'd have found out just what he had to offer.

He kept his beauty until well into middle age; having read
his story, almost all of which came as a complete surprise, I find
myself wondering whether he kept a portrait of himself in the
attic.

I knew he'd tried on my knickers. Our mother knew it, too. She thought it was natural curiosity and something he would grow out of. We didn't tell our father. I had no idea he dreamed about being submissive, or that he thought submission went with being female. If I had known that I would have disabused him and he might have been spared a lot of what happened. Of course, he probably wouldn't have wanted to be spared it.

Chapter 5
Author: James & Lucy

Next morning, we rose late. Ben watched as I took off the cotton baby doll panties and the top. 'I'll wash your things, ready for your return. If you are able to return. Which I hope you will.'

I picked up the French knickers. 'I'd like to take these with me?'

'Of course. They are yours.'

I bathed while he prepared breakfast. Then I put on the knickers, and over them I dressed in my hitch-hiking gear—men's jeans, a man's shirt, men's socks.

Ben gave me a piece of paper on which he had written his address and his telephone number. 'I'll drive you to the outskirts of Minehead.'

'It's a long way.'

'I would drive much further for you. I would go to the ends of the earth.'

His hand rested on my thigh all the way there, my own lying on top of it. About five miles outside the town he turned off into a narrow lane. After half a mile there was a gate into a field, and in front of the gate a space off the road. He pulled in. He put his arms round me and kissed me. His tongue found mine. We embraced for some time.

'You'd better go now,' he said. 'I'll be thinking of you.'

'And I of you.'

'Do your parents open your mail?'

'My father might.'

'I won't write, then. But you can write to me. If you want to.'

I kissed him again. He unloaded my rucksack and put it on the road.

When I looked back, he was still watching me. I blew him

a kiss.

The sun was still shining. At midday I bought a ham and tomato sandwich and a cup of tea in a small cafe. I had been thinking about the lies I was going to have to tell. At five I went to the Youth Hostel and sat outside, waiting.

The others turned up an hour later. 'Well! What happened to you?'

'I was waylaid,' I said. 'A woman picked me up. She lives on her own. She asked me to stay another night.'

'Oh, yes. Sure.' We all talked about girls. None of us had ever done the things we talked about.

I said, 'She gave me something to remember her by.' And, looking around to make sure we were unobserved, I unbuttoned my jeans and flashed the knickers at them.

That was envy I was looking at. Envy pure and unadorned. I was The Man. I had done what they only dreamed of doing, and done it so well that I had been asked to stay an extra night for a repeat performance. I said, 'She asked me to stay the week. If I could have got hold of you, I would have done.'

For the rest of that trip, I was aware of standing a little apart from my companions. I was held in a new esteem. They wanted details. Descriptions of the woman; an account of how it felt to be in her. My imagination readily provided them.

I did feel guilty but I had no choice. I could not say I had been penetrated three times; that I had been tossed off and my cock sucked by a man; that I had sucked him off in my turn. You could not, at that time, admit to being queer.

Of course, I should have known they would not keep their mouths shut. When we were back at school others asked to hear the same stories I had told them. I obliged.

It did not stop there. The story spread. One day, Katie said,

'These knickers I've been hearing about. Have you still got them?'

I stared at her, open-mouthed. She said, 'Give them to me. I'll wash them for you.'

Still I couldn't speak.

'Jimmy. You can't keep a pair of dirty knickers. It isn't hygienic.'

Three days later she handed them back, washed and ironed. 'I hope you keep them hidden. We don't want our Mam finding them.'

It spread even further. My relationship with my father improved. One day he said, 'Did you enjoy your walking holiday?' I wasn't sure what he was getting at but then he patted me on the back. 'Good lad,' he said. 'A chip off the old block.'

The girls in the High School next door knew about it, too. One day I was walking back from the shop where I'd bought a meat pie for lunch and two girls nudged each other and sniggered. They both said, 'Hello, Jimmy' as I passed.

And then there was Margaret Holmes.

Margaret was the talk of the boys' Sixth Form. Like me, she had stayed on for an extra year, planning on a Cambridge scholarship. She looked like an angel—polite, demure, sweet even. Her father was a sea-going engineer and often away from home; her mother was a town councillor, an amateur dramatics producer and a leading light in a number of civic societies of one kind or another, so Margaret spent a lot of evenings at home alone. The word spread by the other girls was that she had the mind of a whore.

I was walking along the road behind the two schools when she suddenly appeared in front of me, walking in the opposite direction. We were on a collision course. I stepped to my right; she stepped to her left. I went left; she went right. When we were about a foot apart I stepped into the road to get out of her way.

She stopped. 'Hey!'

I stopped, too.

She said, 'Are you avoiding me?'

'I was making room for you to pass.'

'Why didn't you ask if I wanted to pass?'

'I'm sorry?'

'Do you like Elvis?'

'Elvis?'

'Presley. Do you like him?'

'Oh. Well. Yes.'

'I just got the new L P. Why don't you come round tonight and we'll play it?'

'Tonight?'

She put a hand on my arm. 'Do you have something better to do?'

'I...no.' That wasn't strictly true; I had an essay to right on the problems caused by the Treaty of Vienna and another about the impact of the Lyrical Ballads when they were first published; but I had another two days before the first had to be in and the second wasn't due till the following Monday. I was only allowed to play records at home at weekends, and not loudly even then. In any case, my queer orientation wasn't set in stone; I did see the point and the attraction of girls. And being able to say I'd spent an evening alone with Margaret Holmes was going to push my reputation among my peers even higher. The final argument was that I absolutely did not want people to suspect that I was queer, and if I refused this chance what else could they possibly think? My reputation as a stud stood on weak foundations, in fact on a lie, and here was an opportunity to make the footings stronger.

'Won't your parents mind?'

'Dad's somewhere off the coast of Nigeria. Mam has to go out at six thirty and she won't be back till after midnight. You could arrive about seven?'

'I...yes. Okay.'

She gave me her address. 'We'll have a nice evening.'

Chapter 6
Author: James's Sister

Iknew Margaret Holmes; she had been in the fourth form at the High School the year I left, so there was no contact between us, but I knew people she knew and I knew the girls who said she was no better than she should have been. It was unfair. Young people at that time were required to lead completely unnatural lives, and that was especially true of the ones clever enough to have passed the 11Plus. They were grammar school boy and high school girl; the world was their oyster. What was expected was that they would study hard, gain qualifications and—the boys at least, and some of the girls—get good jobs as a result. In their twenties, they would marry a suitable person and raise a family. Until then they must put all thoughts of the opposite sex out of their minds.

But at eighteen you are a sexual animal. Shakespeare knew that; he got Anne Hathaway pregnant when he was that age which suggests they were probably at it when he was younger than Margaret and Jimmy when they got together. When Romeo and Juliet were their age, they were already dead. What was expected was not reasonable.

Margaret was very highly sexed, and she was one of those who had watched Jimmy on the cricket field, or when he passed by on his bike. Boys and girls from the two schools met outside at lunch time to chat about things that, looking back, would seem puerile. Jimmy was never one of them. He spent his lunchtimes throwing a ball around, running, or in the school library. I picture Margaret joining the others and wondering whether Jimmy would ever turn up to be flirted with. I imagine the lust growing inside her. Boys were supposed to feel horny and girls were not; I can tell you, speaking from the heart, that that is not real life.

I have inserted this chapter into Jimmy's narrative because I felt Margaret needed to be defended from what may look like charges of unbridled sexuality. There will be more interventions. If you don't like them, ignore the chapters headed "Author: James's Sister."

PS: Now, when I read the next chapter again, I wonder whether I was wrong; whether Margaret really was, in fact, the absolute wanton so many took her to be. She certainly surrendered her virginity with stunning alacrity. It is, of course, possible that she never meant to go that far but was blown away by Jimmy's prowess, taught to him by Ben. IJ met her and so I know that she is now a respectable woman, married for the second time and a grandmother six times over. He felt there was little point in asking her now to explain what had motivated her then, and I think he's right. In any case, the conversation I report in Chapter Twelve is probably as accurate an account of what she was really up to as we are ever going to get.

Chapter 7
Author: James

I wrote to Ben that afternoon, one of a series of letters I sent him, telling him I missed him. I didn't mention Margaret.

Telling my parents where I was going was probably not a good idea. A few times I'd spent a couple of hours with my friend Keith at the house of our joint friend Michael. All three of us had university aspirations, much less common then than now even among grammar school boys, and we'd used the time to discuss essays we had to write and hammer out the doubts and failures to understand that one or other of us might have. Michael's house also had the advantage, which mine and Keith's did not, that his parents had not yet got round to installing a phone, so if my parents wanted to get in touch with me they couldn't.

I told them that's where I was going and at six thirty I got my bike out and set off for Margaret's house. It would take me half an hour to ride there.

When I arrived, I cycled straight past because there was a car in the small driveway. We didn't have a car but the Holmeses clearly did and it looked as though Mrs Holmes hadn't gone out after all. I stopped at the end of the road and wondered what to do. Then the front door opened and a woman came out, clearly in a hurry, with Margaret standing in the doorway behind her. The woman gave Margaret a quick peck on the cheek, said something and then jumped in the car and drove off. Margaret was looking straight at the place where I sat on my bike. She went to the garage door, opened it and gave me what was clearly meant as a meaningful look. Then she went back into the house. She left the door ajar.

What I was being told to do was clear enough. I cycled over, wheeled my bike into the garage and closed the door behind it. Then I walked through the front door. Margaret was just inside, waiting to close it behind me. She turned and stood, inches away. I had been allotted a role and I had better play it out. I kissed her on the lips. She was not offended. There wasn't much doubt that she joined in the kiss. She took my hand and led me into the sitting room.

There was a Dansette record player on a table. She took a record out of its sleeve, put it on the Dansette and started it. I was churned up with excitement; I'm not sure I registered at the time what record it was and I certainly can't remember now. It was probably Elvis but it might have been *La Bohème* for all the impression it made on me. She took my hand again and sat down; I had little choice but to sit beside her. She turned her face to mine.

What struck me then and comes back to me now was the sweet, simple friendliness of her smile.

I knew from listening to boys older than I was what to expect now. The boy would spend the evening trying to get the girl's knickers off and she would spend it resisting. He would put his hand up her skirt; if she wore stockings (there were no tights then) he might if she were sufficiently excited get as far as the bare skin between stocking top and knicker elastic; if he were really lucky he might get to touch the knickers themselves, though at the side and not in front. That would be it. When he finally had to give up and go home he would be frustrated but also relieved.

Relieved because the Pill was still a year or two away, and pregnancy was death to all aspirations. If you got a girl pregnant, you married her. Instead of going to university, you got a job. You lived the early years of marriage either in hand to mouth poverty or the home of your wife's resentful parents and it was difficult to know which would be worse.

We all knew this because we had seen it, in boys and girls very little older than ourselves.

Which made what happened that evening both surprising and scary.

I put my arm round her, because I could see that it was expected. She snuggled into me. I kissed her—that, too, was expected. She kissed me back. Her lips were warm and soft; her tongue, when it snaked into my mouth, was warm, wet and inviting.

She broke away and said, 'I know what they say about me, Jimmy. I'm not a tart. I've never had a boyfriend before.'

Clearly, a boyfriend is what she felt I was.

She kissed me again. I put my hand on her knee beneath the hem of the cotton dress in blue and white checks that was the summer uniform of the High School girls and began to slide it up her bare leg.

She was not resisting at all. Clearly more was expected; you had to go on till the girl made you stop; I knew that. Otherwise she would tell her friends insulting things about your sexuality, and her friends would tell your friends, and you'd never hear the end of it. I put both hands behind her and pulled down the zip on the back of her dress. I expected her to tell me to stop. Really, I wanted her to tell me to stop, because then our future would be protected and my reputation unthreatened. If anything, she'd tell people that I was "too fast".

She did not tell me to stop.

I pulled the dress forward off her shoulders. She shrugged her way out of it and put her now naked arms around my neck. She pulled me to her. She kissed me.

More was expected. It was expected from me. But when I tried to unhook her brassiere, I couldn't do it. She reached behind her, brushed my hands out of the way and let the bra fall down her arms before throwing it over her shoulder.

The lessons I had had from Ben came back to me. I rolled my thumb across one of her nipples and heard her moan. I kissed it; I blew on it; I drew it into my mouth and let my tongue play with it. The moans became louder. Where Elvis had got to on his track list, if Elvis is who it was, I could not have said.

My left hand stayed with her breast; my right began to rub her tummy in gentle circles. I don't know whether she pulled me down or whether I laid her flat on her back, but flat on her back she was. In danger of falling off the sofa, I put a knee between her legs. Then I put the other one there. Her eyes were closed. Her moans had not stopped. I moved my knees a little apart and her legs moved with them. I lifted her skirt to her waist. She grabbed her slip and pulled it out of the way, too. I put my hand between

45

her legs, right in the front where boy's school wisdom said it would never be allowed. There was a slickness beneath the navy blue cotton. I began to rub.

'You'll smear my knickers,' she said. 'My mother will want to know how it happened.'

More than half in hope, I said, 'You want me to stop?'

'No, Jimmy. I don't want you to stop. I want you to take them off me.'

People imagine that a man who likes men will be put off by the sight of the female vulva. I wasn't. I thought it was beautiful, and so was the musky scent it gave off. I had no idea what oral sex with a woman should be like or how it was conducted, but I knew from my time with Ben how useful the mouth could be. I lowered my face and kissed her there. She let out an astonished shriek, seized my head in her hands and pressed it to her. I ran my tongue the length of her slit. You couldn't describe the inarticulate sounds of pleasure she was making now as moans. I ran my tongue up and down again. And then again. Her hips were jerking up and down.

I sat up, laid my hand flat and let one finger enter. There was no need of Vaseline here; she carried her own lubrication in plenty. I inserted another finger. 'Oh Jesus,' she gasped. 'Oh, God. Wait, Jimmy.'

She pushed my chest, hard. I breathed a sigh of relief as I stood up. She stood, too. She pulled the dress over her head and stepped out of the slip. All she had on now was her white ankle socks. That naked body was beautiful. I was as hard as I had ever been with Ben. She said, 'I'll be right back,' and ran out of the room and up the stairs.

She was back in moments carrying a towel. 'Why haven't you taken your clothes off?' As I did so, she folded the towel and laid it on the sofa, right where her bottom had been. She lay down on it. 'We don't want to make a mess, do we?'

There had been a change in me. I no longer even half wanted to stop and I wasn't sure I could if I had to. Had she asked me to, I think I might well have pressed on. The question did not in any case arise. I lifted myself on one elbow and placed myself at the entrance with the other hand. I pushed forward. I was inside her.

A young man inside a girl for the first time should have been incontinent. I should have been unable to hold myself back for more than a few seconds. But I was not a total beginner; I had been through what I had with Ben. I began to move in her the way he had moved inside me. It lasted two minutes, three minutes. And then, as I felt the moment on me and the uprush of seed beginning, sense reasserted itself. I pulled out. In a frenzied twitching I spent on her firm white tummy.

She wrapped her arms round me and held me tight. I was kissing her. She was kissing me. She pressed her mouth to my ear. 'Thank you for not doing it inside me.' Then she put my hand back between her legs. 'Finish me, Jimmy.'

I worked her with my fingers. I didn't really know what a clitoris was, but her passionate convulsions when I touched the right spot guided me to it. She came in an endearing flurry of swearwords.

We lay still. I can't know what was in her mind, but in mine was pleasure at what I had just experienced and surprise at what I had done. Everyone believed that I was experienced with women. And now—a little, anyway—I was.

Some time later, she sat up. She was studying the place between her legs. 'Look,' she said. I looked. She was pointing at the blood on the top of one thigh. 'You see?' she said. 'I told you I wasn't a slut. You're my first, Jimmy.'

Chapter 8
Author: James

I know, looking back, that that was a critical time for me. It's easy to think that we are formed at an early age and nothing can change it, but it isn't true. I had grown up wanting to wear girl's clothes and submit like a girl. Okay, so that made me a queer. But now I was seeing Margaret outside school every weekday lunchtime and going to her house once, twice, sometimes even three times a week and while I was there so long as she didn't have her period I was making love to her. So that made me straight.

If Margaret had been my only sexual partner, I would probably have seen the two days with Ben as an aberrant teenage interlude, to be put behind me.

But she wasn't.

Summer was over and autumn was here. Like the rest of the high school girls, Margaret had changed out of her cotton dresses and into the dark blue gym slips that were their winter uniform. The cricket season was over. Athletics were in full flow.

British hypocrisy was as evident in sport as it was in matters of sexuality. As athletes, we were amateurs. No-one paid us. It wasn't just us. Wimbledon was a tennis tournament for amateurs only. There was a huge network of amateur football clubs; star players who worked in London but played for leading clubs in County Durham like Bishop Auckland would travel all the way home once or twice a week (and there was no motorway then) for training and to play, not for money but for simple love of the game. Or so they said. Athletics also had its little tricks.

In the club house each week there would be posters advertising upcoming meetings. Against each event would be a list of the prizes for first, second and third places, with their value.

First place: Silver Cup, £5. Second place: Silver Rose Bowl, £2 10s.
Third place: Silver Plate, £1. 10s

Five pounds was a lot of money in those days. A working

man's wife might have no more than that as her housekeeping budget for the week.

When you won, you were presented with your prize in public. In private afterwards, a conversation along these lines took place: "That's a nice rose bowl. Would you like to sell it?" "How much?" "Two pounds ten." "Okay." And you went home with your illegal prize money in your pocket.

I picked my meets carefully, looking for the ones with relatively modest prizes that would not attract the big names. Derek Ibbotson was the leading English miler at the time and I knew I wouldn't be winning any first prizes with him in the field. I was a good miler and very fair over three miles and I had a steady flow of extra pocket money. My mother was not interested in silver rose bowls or plates and although I won a few I never took one home. My picture would sometimes appear in the local paper proudly holding up my prize before I had traded it in and that was enough.

Reggie was a tireless factotum of the club. People said he'd been a good long jumper in his day, but his day had been twenty years earlier. Now he devoted his time to helping and encouraging the young athletes. He spent more time encouraging the boys than the girls. He had a car and sometimes he would offer a lift home.

On the day I'm thinking of, I had taken first place and pocketed a fiver and I was feeling pretty good. Reggie offered to run me home and I thought that was better than two bus changes. I'd noticed the way Reggie looked at me, especially in the changing rooms where he popped up more often than might have seemed necessary, and that might have put me off the idea of getting into his car. It didn't.

He drove to his house and not to mine. 'Come in for a coffee.' I knew what was going on. I was at least half erect and in my stomach I had that feeling people call butterflies.

There was no Mrs Reggie. It was a nice house, clean and well appointed, and he lived in it alone. In the kitchen he turned towards me and pressed me against the wall. His face was inches from mine. He said, 'I've been watching you.'

'I know you have.'

'I've heard all about Margaret Holmes.'

'Oh?'

'I think that's a front. I think you're one of us.'

'Oh?'

He kissed me. I let him. He put his hand on the front of my jeans. I was now rock hard. He said, 'Let's go to bed.'

'Okay.'

He was efficient and he was good. He took complete charge and I submitted. He fucked me long and he fucked me hard. I didn't know at that time about the prostate and how it responds to a cock rubbing it from inside. Not knowing why I was coming didn't prevent it from happening.

Then we got dressed and had the coffee he'd promised, and then he took me home.

Reggie's lifts to and from athletic meets continued. Sometimes he would also bring other people back but he always left my drop-off till last and we always went to his house before mine and he always fucked me.

And that was how my life proceeded. I fucked Margaret, who was a girl; I was fucked by Reggie, who was a man. Nowadays I suppose I'd be called bisexual but we didn't have that word (or that concept) in those days. You were queer or you were straight. I wasn't sure which I was, though Reggie had no such doubts. 'You're as queer as a coot, Jimmy.' I was no ornithologist and I didn't (still don't) know why that particular bird was thought to be homosexual. In spring there were always plenty of little fledgling coots paddling furiously across lakes behind their mothers.

I enjoyed the way I was living my life and was happy for it to continue. It ended when I made Margaret pregnant.

I had never graduated to condoms, which then we called "johnnies" and which in those days were less easy to get hold of than they are now. A youth of my age could face questioning when he asked the barber for something for the weekend. Margaret had warned me that she had missed a period. The warning was more serious when she missed a second one.

Mr Holmes cut short a trip to Africa (with great loss of earnings and irritation to his employers, as he made clear) and flew home from Lagos. He came to see my father. Then I was brought in and confronted with the results of my seduction of his daughter. I was too much the gentleman, and too fond of Margaret, to correct this view.

Mr Holmes said, 'I'm not going to ruin Margaret's life for one mistake.' One? We'd been at it like rabbits. 'I won't make her marry you and in fact I won't let her. She'll have the baby and it will be adopted. The school is prepared to take her back next year. She'll be a year behind, but she can still get to university. I want two things from you and then I never want to see you or hear about you again. The first thing you have to do is stay away from her. And the second is to find a university for yourself that is not Cambridge, because that's where she'll be going and I don't want you near her. Understand?'

My father said, 'Now wait a minute...' but I interrupted. 'That's okay, Dad. I've been thinking of applying to Bristol anyway.'

He was giving me a very strange look. 'Okay, son. If you're sure that's all right with you.'

Mr Holmes said, 'You're getting off very lightly. Stay away from my daughter.' And he left.

After he'd gone my mother wanted to get into the conversation but my father sent her away. To me he said, 'Bristol. Isn't that where...'

'I was there in the summer. Hitch hiking.'

'And that's where she was. The woman with the knickers.'

I nodded.

'How old is she, Jimmy?'

'I don't know. Younger than you and Mam, I think.'

'Married?'

'She's divorced.'

'Oh. Well. She'll know how to look after herself, at any rate. You're better off with an older woman. Till you want to find someone to settle down with. Now go and talk to your mother. Agree with everything she says. And don't tell her why you want to go to Bristol. In fact, don't mention this conversation at all.'

'No, Dad.'

'He's right, you know. You have got off lightly. It's not just the girl's life that would have been ruined.' He laughed. 'Older women. Knickers as souvenirs. You're a chip off the old block, all right.'

A couple of days later, he put a box of Durex in my hand. 'Hide those. Don't let your mother see them. When you need more, tell me.'

Every four of five days, I took one out of the box and threw it away. When the box was almost empty, I told him I needed a refill.

'Bloody hell,' he said. 'You're getting more than I am.' He said it with pride, though, and a replacement box arrived before the day was out.

The day after Mr Holmes's visit, I was told to go to the Headmaster's office. 'I've had a very angry phone call from Doctor Comstock about you, Carlton.' Dr Comstock was the headmistress of the girls' high school.

'Yes, sir?'

'I understand you have got one of her innocent charges in an interesting condition.'

'I'm afraid so, sir.'

'Yes. Well. Doctor Comstock has asked me to instruct you to stay away from all of her girls. And I am so instructing you. Is that clear?'

'Yes, sir.'

'If I hear that you have so much as nodded to a High

School girl on the other side of the road, you will not like the consequences. Is *that* clear?'

'Yes, sir.'

'In school hours or out of them, Carlton.'

'Yes, sir.'

'Hmm. Well. Good. Have you never heard of prophylactics, Carlton?'

'Sir?'

'Contraceptives, man. Johnnies.'

'Oh. Yes, sir.'

'Then why didn't you use one? *Coitus interruptus* is not a reliable form of family planning. As you and this no doubt blameless maid now know.'

'Yes, sir.'

'The good Doctor also raised the question of university.' Our head did not have a doctorate and he seemed to find something amusing in Dr Comstock's use of the title. 'She wants you to promise to steer clear of Cambridge.'

'Yes, sir.'

'That's a shame. You're one of our brightest pupils. You do plan to go to university?'

'Yes, sir. I thought of Bristol, sir.'

'Bristol. A good university.'

'Yes, sir.'

'Very well, Carlton. That will be all. Remember what I've told you.'

'Yes, sir.'

My reputation was, if anything, enhanced. Not only had I bedded a woman twice my age; I had also got a girl in the family way and walked away from it without personal damage. I was the boy, all right. A real Jack the Lad. No-one would ever have imagined I might be going to bed with men, too.

I was, though. Reggie and I weren't a weekly coupling or

even always a monthly one but we did come together without our clothes on. I enjoyed it and I believe he did, too. We continued all the way through that year and a lot of the next.

Nor was he the only one.

I was on Northumberland Street when I saw on the face of a man walking towards me a look that wasn't hard to interpret. He wanted eye contact and I let him have it but I walked straight past him.

About fifty yards further on, I paused and looked back. He had stopped, too, and was watching me. When he saw me looking he started walking back towards me. I stayed where I was. He said, 'Haven't we met?' and I said, 'I don't know. Where?' and he said, 'Well, never mind. I'm staying in the hotel opposite the station. Do you want to come to my room?'

That's how simple it was. When we got to his room he hung the Do Not Disturb sign outside the door and put the safety chain on the door. Then he kissed me. I suppose he could tell my inclination from the way I held myself. He said, 'You like to take the girl's part, do you?'

'I suppose I do, yes.'

'How far do you go?'

'Have you got any Vaseline?'

'I certainly have.'

'I go all the way, then.'

And I did. Reggie always had me face down on the bed and with this man I insisted on taking it the other way, lying on my back with my legs raised and looking up at him as he did me. I was conscious of the risk of being seen with a strange man so when it was over I said, 'We'll leave separately, shall we?'

'Sure. I'll give you a ten minute start.'

Now I knew how to pick a man up. He was not the last. I've always found gays to be sexually omnivorous and I was no exception. Even though I still told myself I wasn't really queer. Not

55

exclusively, anyway.

There was no contact between me and Margaret after her father's visit. Then, seven months later, she wrote to me.

In the letter was a photograph.

Dear Jimmy

I thought you'd like to have this picture of our daughter, when she was three days old and before she was taken away from me. It's so sad to think I'll never see her again. I feel bereft.

I still love you, Jimmy and I hope I'll see you again some day. My parents don't know I'm sending this so please don't write back, but don't forget me, either.

Love

M

xxxxxxx

It wasn't until I read that that I really took in the enormity of what we had done. We had brought into being a new life, a whole new person, and she was gone somewhere we would not be told to be raised by people we would never meet. They might tell her she was adopted and they might not. Even if they did, she would never know who we were, or why we had let her go.

I felt a complete shit.

Half way through the last school term of the year I applied to Bristol and was accepted. My extracurricular activities had taken their toll on my work—my A Level grades weren't as good as expected and I wouldn't have got to Cambridge even if I hadn't promised not to go there. I wrote to Ben and he wrote back using the words he had said he would.

Chapter 9
Author: James & Lucy

When I arrived at Ben's house, I found a woman with him.

'Don't worry,' she said. 'Ben hasn't got married. I'm Belinda. His sister.'

Ben said, 'We thought your parents might bring you so Belinda came to pretend to be my wife.'

'They don't have a car,' I said.

'Well, never mind. Belinda's been shopping for you so it hasn't been a complete waste of time.'

Belinda left soon after that. Ben pressed her to stay for dinner but she said she had to get back. She kissed him on the cheek and me on the forehead. 'He's missed you,' she said to me. 'Be good to him.'

We went upstairs, with Ben insisting on carrying my suitcase. I'd heard the expression "walk-in wardrobe" but never realised till now that that meant a wardrobe you could actually walk in to. Like a little room. There were two rails; his clothes hung from the one on the right and on the left-hand rail were skirts and dresses. 'Those are yours,' he said.

Then he showed me the two chests of drawers. Once again, the one on the right was his. In the other were knickers of every description, blouses, t-shirts, tops, nightdresses and pyjamas. I was stunned. Not just stunned; I was projected back into my girly days. If I wanted, I could become Ben's submissive girl all over again.

I wanted.

Ben said, 'I'll put your case in the next room. That will be your room when you have people over and you can keep all your normal clothes in there.'

'Those are my man clothes,' I said. 'These are my normal clothes.'

He smiled and kissed me. 'I'll leave you to freshen up. I'll go down and get started on dinner.'

I took my clothes off and started on the knicker drawer. I was spoilt for choice. I settled on a pair of pink satin briefs. Then I put on a pink cotton blouse and a red miniskirt that came half way down my thighs. I felt like a princess.

Ben was making a beef and tomato sauce for pasta. The kitchen smelt strongly of garlic. He turned to look at me as I came through the door. Ben wasn't one of those men I had picked up during the past eighteen months and discarded after a one afternoon stand. The look on his face was one of deep affection. I said, 'Worth waiting for?'

He crossed the room, took me in his arms and kissed me. 'You look sensational.'

'You've spent a lot of money.'

'I *have* a lot of money. Who better to spend it on than you?'

I leaned my head against his chest. Whatever I'd been doing since I'd seen him last, I was home now. I snuggled against him.

As well as the pasta, Ben had made a big mixed salad. Salad to my mother meant hard boiled eggs, lettuce, cucumber and radishes served with Heinz Salad Cream. It did not include olives, feta cheese, peppers and spring onions, as Ben's did, and nor did it come with his vinaigrette. We drank a bottle of wine between us and we followed the main course with a ripe camembert.

We were shy and restrained around each other. I knew now that men who preferred men could be promiscuous and given to one night stands and I did not ask Ben whether he had picked up any hitchhikers since me because I didn't want to know. Nor did I tell him about Reggie or any of the other men I had been to bed with; I certainly wasn't going to mention Margaret or our baby.

We did talk about my athletics, my A Levels, the books we had both been reading, the books I wanted to read, the books I should read and my first year syllabus.

Afterwards, he made coffee and we drank it with whisky sitting on the same sofa as the one on which he had taught me how to fellate him. I decided I had to do something to remove this caution that existed between us.

When the coffee was over, I sat on his knee. I put my arms round his neck and kissed him. He said, 'You still feel the same way?'

'No,' I said. 'I feel much more strongly.'

'What do you want to do now?'

'Do you remember your fantasy? Well, I've got one, too. In my fantasy I'm upstairs, lying in bed in my nightie and nothing else. A burglar comes in. He sees this beautiful young girl who's just had a bath and looks so sweet and he has to have her. I struggle, but he's bigger than me and he overpowers me. Then he has his way.'

'You little minx.'

'Yes.'

'I've had a shower installed since you were last here.'

'He sees this beautiful young girl who's just had a shower and looks so sweet and he has to have her.'

'I'll give you ten minutes to have your shower and get ready.'

I kissed him again, jumped up and ran upstairs. As before, when I was with him I wasn't a man—I was a young girl.

Although I had made it up on the spur of the moment, my fantasy did the trick. After I'd resisted a little but not too much and he'd held me down while he filled my bottom from the biggest jar of Vaseline anyone has ever seen and then filled it again with his lovely big, hard cock, and finally filled it one last time with a volume of semen that suggested he'd been saving it since our last frolic together, the distance between us had been closed. I fell asleep in his arms.

Next morning, I had to register at university so I dressed like a male student and not like a girl, but under the jeans I put on a snug pair of cotton knickers. It meant I'd have to go into a cubicle and sit down to wee, but girls always have to do that.

Ben told me that I was embarking on Freshers' Week, that I would be expected to socialise and should do so, that he would have food available if I wanted it but would not feel hurt if I failed to be home for meals or to say goodnight (or even failed to come home at all, though he would like me to call so he knew I was all right) and that if I wanted to bring any of my new acquaintances home I was welcome to do so and I should call him Uncle and take them to "my" room.

He also checked that I had enough money and, although I did, he put twenty pounds in my hand. That was a huge amount of money in those days. 'Don't go short of anything,' he said. 'Make a splash. Let them know you're there.'

Young people don't have a great deal of faith in the wisdom of old people, and the Jimmy Carlton I have been writing about—the boy who was eighteen when this story started and is only nineteen at the point we have now reached—would have seen the James Carlton who is writing this story forty-seven years later as a very old man indeed. L P Hartley said, "The past is another country. They do things differently there." They do. And the reason they do things differently is that they are different people. When I look back from here at the things I did then, I see them from a perspective that was not available to the young man I was.

I have made Margaret sound like a slut. She was not. She was a lovely girl who thought about sex most of her waking minutes and dreamed about sex most of her sleeping hours. In that she was no different from me or most of the young people around us. What was different was that she identified a boy—me—with whom she could put her dreams into practice, and she did it. As a result, she bore a beautiful little girl whom she had to give up and she was labelled "bad" and saw girls she had thought of as friends told by their mothers to stay away from her. A terrible price to pay.

We think of the Victorian years as a time of sexual repression and hypocrisy, but they were no more so than Britain in the Nineteen Fifties. At the very age when humans are designed to be most sexually active, they were expected not even to think about sex. When boys should have been learning to coexist with girls, they were segregated—in schools, in clubs, in almost every way. A hard workout on the sports field followed by a cold shower were thought to be sufficient answer to burgeoning lust. They are not. Strong desires that are repressed do not disappear—they emerge in unnatural ways. I had a strange idea of sexual pleasure. But so did everyone, though the dreams of each were different.

I wish the James Carlton that I am now as I approach the end of this wonderful life could have whispered advice in the ear of the Jimmy Carlton I was then.

But, even if I could have, he would not have listened.

Today, going to university is a general thing. In those days, we were a small and privileged group. Most of us were away from home for the first time in our lives and considered ourselves free to do the things we wanted to do because no-one from home was watching. Nobody around you knew you when you were growing up and you can reinvent yourself. You can be the person you want to be and not the one you have been. That can, of course, be disastrous and for some people it was.

Not for me.

One or two male students made it clear, if I wanted to take the message, that they were available. I ignored them. I was going to be faithful to Ben and, anyway, I didn't want to be seen as queer. Girls were a different matter. I acquired a girlfriend in that first week and when we broke up after three months I got another one. And then another. I had sex with all of them and word got around among the female students that I, unlike most of the other young men there, knew what I was doing. Usually we'd go to the girl's digs, but Ben was away on business (often abroad) about one week in four and then they came to "my" place. They never met my Uncle Ben. He told me I was free to invite people home but, apart from the girls and one at a time, I didn't. I wasn't going to hold a party while he was away because student parties ended with cigarette butts trodden into the carpet and rings from glasses on the furniture and I wasn't going to do that to Ben. And I didn't want a crowd of students to see Ben because it only needed one of them to spot his sexual orientation for people to start asking questions about me.

My father had sent me to university with a big box of johnnies and when that ran out I bought more. I wasn't going to be responsible for another illegitimate child and nor was I going to risk the degree I'd worked so hard to put myself in line for.

The Vietnam War was hotting up, with US forces doubling and doubling again, and it was a time of great student unrest. The idea of marches and sit-ins left me cold. I lost one girlfriend because I refused to go on demos with her but I didn't care. I wasn't at university to change the world; I was there to secure my future and to satisfy my lover.

In the three weeks out of four that he was home, if I was there at the right time we'd talk, have dinner together, fool around and go to bed. When it was just him and me I always wore girl's clothes. If I got home when he was already in bed I'd take a shower, put on a nightie or a pair of baby dolls and get into bed where he would be waiting. It might seem daft that I always put my night things on, bearing in mind that he would take them off again, but I liked having him undress me and I knew he liked it, too.

When Ben was stroking my legs he'd say how good it was that they weren't very hairy (as his were, for example). He said it often enough that I said, 'It's a shame I have too much hair to wear stockings.' Belinda visited a few days later with suspender belts and stockings and showed me how to shave my legs and how to put the stockings on straight. She said, 'Always put the belt on under the knickers. Then when Ben takes the knickers off you you'll still look sexy. Apart from which, if you have the suspenders over the knickers, how will you get them down when you go to the bathroom?' Clearly there was a lot of communication between Ben and his sister but he never went to her house because her husband didn't want a queer man near their children.

Some nights when Ben was making love to me he must

have realised that I'd been active earlier that same day but he never said anything. And I didn't care because what I had with Ben was different from what I had with girls—then I had to take the lead but with Ben I lay back and let him take what he wanted. I wanted it too.

One afternoon when he was on the sofa I knelt before him, unzipped his trousers, took him out of his pants and blew him. I often did that, but this time when he warned me he was about to come and tried to move my head I pushed his hands away and kept working on him till he came in my mouth. I sat back on my heels and smiled at him.

'Lucy,' he said. 'Why didn't you let me take it out?'

'I wanted you,' I said. 'I wanted you to come in my mouth. I love you.' And I knew that I did.

When I said that, he leaned forward, grabbed me in his arms and hauled me backwards in a great bear hug. He kissed me. Then, 'Hell's teeth, Luce,' he said. 'Your mouth doesn't taste very nice.'

I laughed. 'It tastes of you.' But I went to the bathroom and swilled mouthwash around to get rid of the taste.

I usually swallowed after that. I always used mouthwash immediately afterwards.

Chapter 10
Author: James & Lucy

In my third year, my loyalty to Ben was tested. One of the history lecturers had asked me to visit him at home for a tutorial. I had a good idea what he wanted, but people I was sure were straight had had the same invitation so what could I do?

We discussed my essay on the causes and outcome of the Hundred Years War and he suggested some further reading that would widen my understanding. He asked if I was interested in working as a teaching assistant while I pursued post-graduate research. I was tempted.

Then he said, 'I bet you have a lovely cock.'

I didn't see any point in dissembling; he'd seen me for what I was. 'I'm afraid it belongs to someone else.'

'Would he share it with me?'

'I wouldn't ask him to.'

'It could mean the difference between a First and an Upper Second. If you want the teaching assistant's job, a First would be a good idea.'

I weighed what he had said. Even if I decided not to stay on, a First would be a great help in whatever I decided to do next. My indecision must have been obvious. When he took my hand I did not resist. I let him pull me to my feet and lead me to the desk. He took a jar of Vaseline out of the desk drawer and handed it to me. Then he dropped his trousers, pulled his underpants to his knees and leaned forward over the desk.

I was stunned. I had assumed he was like the other men I'd had and wanted to fuck me and not the other way round. I knew what to do, though. One of the girlfriends I had had the previous year had dropped hints continually about being buggered until I did it to her. We did it several more times before she decided I was no longer the person she wanted to be with.

He talked dirty to me the whole time I was getting him ready. When I was in him, the filthy talk increased. While I was doing it I felt like a man and not like a girl and that persuaded me that I was not being unfaithful to Ben. I played with him while I sodomised him and he came all over the leather top. I could tell how much he liked it and I gave it to him hard.

He became a fairly constant part of my life for a few months. Sometimes he just wanted to suck me (and he always swallowed) and sometimes he wanted me in him.

I got my First.

B en said, 'What are you going to do now?'
'I haven't decided.'
'Not many people get a First.'
'No.'
'Have you thought of going on?'
'They've made the offer. But...'

T he big companies had sent their people to interview students. When my degree was known, I had offers from British Petroleum, Guest Keen and Nettlefold and the BBC among others. The BP job was in London and GKN in Birmingham. I said, 'The BBC say while I'm a trainee I can choose whether I want to be in Portman Square or here. In Bristol.'

He looked at me without speaking.

I said, 'I need to know, Ben.'

'To know?'

I was exasperated that he could be so dense. 'To *know*. I've been here three years. Do you still want me? Or have you had enough?'

'Oh, Lucy. Oh, my darling.' He wrapped his arms around me. 'How can you doubt me?'

Relief so deep I thought I might fall. 'The BBC it is, then.'

I n those days, the BBC existed for its broadcasters and its listeners and viewers. It was not the management-dominated organisation it has become. It had not yet lost sight of the reasons it existed. I loved it there.

Over time, I had come to know Ben's background. The conversations were fragmented and happened at different times and sometimes they were oblique, more hints than actual statements; for convenience I will reproduce them here as though they happened on one single evening, although in reality what follows emerged over the four years from my first arrival as an undergraduate to my departure from Bristol for London after a year of BBC training.

'Most homos are promiscuous. They put themselves about. They'll take their clothes off with anyone. Even when two queers live together in a permanent relationship, like you and me, they still have one night stands with anyone who asks. It isn't loving and it isn't faithful but it's how it is. And most homo sex does not involve penetration. There's more masturbation and sucking and rimming than sodomy.'

'Rimming?'

'Licking someone's arse.'

'Oh. Good grief. We've never...'

'No. And we won't. I don't like it.'

'It doesn't sound very nice, I must say.'

'I don't doubt that licking a woman can be an enjoyable thing to do, though I've never tried it, but I don't believe a man's backside would taste very nice and that's that.'

'Have you ever done anything? With a woman, I mean?'

'No. I know you have because you reek of cheap perfume some nights when you come home but there's no need to talk about it. I prefer the male body.'

'My male body, I hope.'

'Of course. I went to a well known school.'

I already knew that because he'd told me where he'd been educated.

'The school took good care of our education. That's how I got to Cambridge. They did not show much interest in what we got up to at night. I was a pretty boy. When I was twelve, one of the senior boys took an amorous interest in me. You'd know him if I told you his name; he became an MP and he was talked about as a coming man but he never made senior office and he resigned his seat very suddenly. There was talk of a scandal but what it was never came out. I can imagine, though.

'The senior boys had their own studies. He told me to go there after prep one evening. He told me to take my clothes off. Then he wanked me till I came. And then he taught me to suck.

'There were a lot of advantages to being a senior boy's pet. And, anyway, there wasn't anything to be done. The housemaster knew what was going on. He called me in one day and gave me a lecture about playing for the team and not exposing the school to gossip. Whatever went on inside the school gates should stay there.

'"My" Senior left that summer. Two days before he left, he said, "Tonight we're going all the way," and we did. That was the first time, my first actual buggery. Then he introduced me to the boy whose pet I was going to be in the autumn. There was no messing about with him; penetration on the first night of the new term and regularly after that.

'The next year I had a new Senior. But I was getting bigger, and I was good at rugby and I learned to box and one evening when I was in his room and he told me to strip off and bend over I said, "No. You do it." He thought I was joking. He found out I wasn't. And that was the end of my time as a pet.

'I didn't have sex again until I got to be a Senior myself. There was a lot more freedom once you had your own room, and no housemaster coming in at odd hours to check up on you. One of the other boys in my year had gone on being bummed all the way through. He was as queer as they come. He asked me to do him and I did. I found I liked being the man. And then I fell for a young boy.'

He sat and stared into the distance for a long time. 'He was a lot like you that time I picked you up,' he said at last. 'The moment I looked at you I thought...Well. Anyway. I took him to my room and I did what had been done to me, but with affection.

I liked him. He was a sweetie. Like you. We still correspond from time to time. I was Best Man at his wedding. I'm godfather to one of his children. We meet whenever I'm in New York. Not for sex; for dinner and to talk about old times. He's with the Embassy there. Be an ambassador soon. They'll start him off in some African shithole, probably. Which is appropriate when you think about it.

'When I was at Cambridge I carried on as before. I went out with a couple of girls but it wasn't for me. It was men, men and more men. One night stands. Cruising public lavatories. Pick-ups in bars. A dangerous life. I needed all my boxing skills sometimes.

'I fell in with a young guy who'd just come up. Good family. Better school even than mine. Produced God knows how many Prime Ministers. He liked to wear women's clothes, too. The Long Vac before my last year I went to stay with his people. Great big spread in Oxfordshire. High wall, iron gate, no strangers passing by. A staff of five people, but he'd walk around in a frock, stockings, silk knickers like those lilac ones Belinda bought for you and no-one said a word. He was a young woman and I was his boyfriend. We shared a bedroom and the maid brought us tea in the morning.'

This silence went on so long, I had to ask, 'What happened to him?'

'He died.'

Another silence. This time I didn't feel able to ask questions.

'The family had another house, in Belgravia.' Each sentence now was coming with a gap between it and the next one. 'You know, the trouble with trying to pass as a woman is the throat... men have an Adam's apple...women don't...he went into a pub... bunch of louts...they picked on him and he answered back.'

'I'm sorry.'

'Yes. That was in 1949. And from then until I saw you, twelve years later, I hadn't had a man. When you've gone, I don't suppose I'll have another.' He blinked away a tear.

'Am I going?'

'Of course you are. The BBC won't leave you here forever. You're destined for great things, Luce.'

He poured two scotches and gave one to me. 'Lift up your skirt and show me what knickers you have on.'

Chapter 11
Author: James

Ben was right about the BBC moving me on. I'd learned to drive and bought a car and now I loaded my stuff into it, including a whole suitcase of women's clothes.

'Stay out of pubs in that gear,' Ben said. He held me tight and kissed me fiercely. 'In Belgravia or out of it.'

Northern boys from ordinary families—that was our time. The world of wealth and family had not yet reasserted itself. People like Melvyn Bragg, Tom Courtenay and Albert Finney were making a name for themselves. In a smaller circle, so was I.

Guy was old school. Marlborough College. Oxford. Recruited by the BBC through a friend of his uncle. In 1939, joined Military Intelligence after a word in the right ear from another uncle, a brigadier. After the war, back to the BBC. He looked like what he was; the well-fed, well educated, expensively dressed son of an old family. He did not look queer. It was best not to in his day. But he knew who all the queers were, and he spotted a new one.

'Come for dinner, old man. We need to know each other better.'

Dinner was at Guy's club. He knew everyone. Men stopped by our table to chat. And to give me the once-over. One or two handed me their cards. 'We should meet.' Guy watched without comment.

His flat in The Albany was walking distance away. 'Let's have coffee at my place, old man.' The way you might invite a girl. Which was fine with me. It went with the French Knickers I wore under my trousers.

'I live here during the week. My wife is in Gloucestershire and the children are away at school.'

On the table, a pot of very good coffee. Cream. Cubes

of dark brown sugar in a bowl. Brandy in a crystal decanter. Two crystal glasses. On the sofa, Guy and me. Side by side.

'So how do you think it's going?'

'?'

'The BBC. Happy in your work?'

'Yes. Thank you.'

'Good. You'll have noticed? Groups of friends? We help each other get on. Those we like.'

I had noticed—the groups of friends, at least. I was too new to have seen how careers could be advanced or held back but I'd take his word for it.

He put his arm round my shoulder. I rested my head against it. He was very close now. He put a hand on my chin, turned my face towards him, kissed me. I joined in. He said, 'Do you have any special likes?'

'I like you to take the lead.'

'Understood, old man. Anything you won't do?'

'I haven't found it yet.'

'Well. Good. Do you think we might be more comfortable in the bedroom?'

We undressed on opposite sides of the bed. His eyes glowed when I left the knickers on. 'Are those for me?'

'Everything you see is for you.'

He was like Ben; another big, commanding man. On the table on his side of the bed, a bottle of oil. Tissues. Vaseline. When he rolled over me, embracing, I felt contained. One hand slipped up my knicker leg to grasp my cock. I put my arms round his back and let my legs part. His tongue slithered into my mouth. Submission. Relief. In both senses.

After he had dealt with my erection, I took his into my mouth. Longer than Ben's. Thicker.

'I want to be inside you.'

I lay back while he rolled the knickers down my legs. He took the Vaseline and prepared me, and then himself. I wrapped my legs round his back and my arms round his shoulders. When he pushed into me it was something he had done before; something he knew how to do. He paused several times in his thrusting, prolonging the moment. Then he came in me.

We lay, locked in each other's arms. His breath smelt sweet. His breathing was steady and regular. Then he rolled me onto my front, went to the bathroom and came back with a warm, damp flannel and a warm towel. He cleaned me. 'Do you have to go?'

'I'd need to be in a taxi at six. I can stay the night. If you want me to.'

'That's good. I always call home about this time. To say goodnight.'

'Go ahead.'

I lay in bed and listened. 'Dinner with a colleague. Some things we had to discuss. No, I'm alone now.' Then, 'Goodnight, darling. I'll see you on Friday. Late, probably. The Audleys? Saturday? Yes, we can do that. All right, darling. Yes, you too.'

From then on, Tuesday night was my night with Guy. I took a pair of baby dolls and a nightie and left one there while I took the other home to wash. He loved that. It really turned him on. What we each did on other nights, neither of us said or asked.

I called the numbers on the cards I had been given when I dined at Guy's club. The men were pleased to get my call and pleased to fuck me, suck me, be sucked or be fucked. I was happier being a bottom, but I'd be a top when that was called for.

Every few weeks I drove to Bristol to see Ben.

And I picked men up in the way I'd learned to do before I left home. I never took anyone back to my flat in the Barbican; if they didn't have somewhere we could go, I found someone else.

Guy told me that I really should have a girlfriend, for the look of the thing and to stop people talking, but I didn't have time for that. It didn't seem to matter; my staff reviews were excellent two years running. I put the picture of Margaret's baby in a frame and stood it on my desk. I let it be known that her mother and I could not marry until her husband divorced her; he was an Arab and a Moslem and was making things very difficult. As Guy said, it was for the look of the thing.

I became a regular walker on Hampstead Heath. I saw other BBC types there. We ignored each other.

Then my parents decided to visit. They would come down by train, spend three nights in the Goring Hotel and visit the Tower, Buckingham Palace, Madame Tussauds. All the tourist things. Things I had never done. Of course, they expected to see me.

'Won't that be a problem?' my secretary asked.

'Why?'

'What are you? Twenty-five? They'll expect you to have a girl with you when you take them to dinner.'

I stared at her. What was she getting at? I knew, though. I was shocked to realise how thin my disguise was.

She patted the back of her head. 'I could come?'

'What? Helen, I...'

'No problem if you don't want me there. Just trying to be helpful.'

My father loved fish and complained that he never got any. 'We live five miles from the sea, and when do I ever see a nice fresh cod?' I booked a table for four at Wheelers. I knew my parents would be there before us; they were always early.

Helen took my hand as I gave my name to the maître d'. She pressed her side against mine. My mother's eyes lit up when she saw the two of us together. 'Lovely to meet you, Helen,' she said when I introduced them. 'You never mentioned Helen, Jimmy.'

Helen turned exasperated eyes to me. 'Men!'

I laughed. We were off to a great start.

My father drooled over the menu. 'Spoilt for choice,' he said.

'We can come again and you can choose something else,' said my mother. She was more interested in Helen. Was she one of these career girls you heard so much about?

'I like to think people are happy with what I do,' Helen said. 'But, really, I'm filling in time. Till I marry and start a family.'

My mother was glowing. 'Do you expect that to be soon?'

Helen gave me a sideways glance. 'It's not my decision alone to make.'

My mother was so happy, I thought she might lay an egg. She produced pictures of the grandchildren Katie had given her and Helen made all the right noises. When Helen went to the bathroom, Mam said, 'She's a lovely girl, Jimmy.'

'Yes. Yes, she is.'

'You could do a lot worse.'

'I could.'

'Leave the boy alone,' said my father. 'He'll get there in his own good time.'

'Thank you,' I said when we'd put my parents in a taxi to take them back to the Goring.

'I enjoyed it. There wasn't enough coffee; apart from that, it was a lovely evening.'

'Not enough coffee? We left a pot standing on the table.'

She was looking straight into my eyes. 'Still,' she said. 'I expect you have some at your place?'

But when we got there, she didn't want coffee. 'It'll make me wee,' she said. 'I have other plans for that part of my anatomy.'

'Helen...'

She put a hand to my cheek. 'I've fancied you like buggery ever since you came to London.' She stifled a giggle. 'I'm sorry. I shouldn't say "buggery" to you, should I? You don't have to do anything you don't want to do, James. Jimmy.' And she giggled again. Then she kissed me. It was a slow, lingering kiss, but the kind that says, "I'm taking charge." That's probably what swung it.

She had a beautiful body. She was almost my height, slim, full breasts, flat stomach and the triangle of hair over her mound was the same golden colour as the hair on her head. She told me to lie on my back, then knelt with one knee on each side of my head and lowered herself towards my mouth, holding the headboard with both hands. The scent of her in arousal was a delight. I put my hands on her hips, pulled her lower and began to lick. She wasn't exactly a screamer but she didn't keep quiet either and I thought, "This will do my reputation with the neighbours no harm". I pushed my tongue between the trembling folds and licked up towards her clitoris. My face was being sprayed by her juices; I could smell them on me. When she came, she ground downwards, then stretched herself out on top of me and hugged me. 'Did you like that, James? Did you like it?'

'It was wonderful.' It was.

Her mouth when she took me into it was as warm and molten as the honeypot I had just licked. When I was ready I made to move, but she stopped me. 'I'm on top.'

She knelt again and guided me into her with her hand. I had never had a woman this way before—her on top, dominant, dictating the pace; me beneath, submitting. I found I could last a lot longer this way. Helen liked that. So did I. She took my hands and placed them on her lovely breasts.

When it was over, she cuddled me. 'The baby on your desk,' she said. 'What happened to it?'

'Her,' I said. 'She was given up for adoption.'

'I thought it must be something like that. That won't happen to me, James. We have the Pill now, and I'm on it. No babies. Not till Mister Right has stood beside me at the altar.'

Katie telephoned. 'So, little brother. Tell me about Helen.'

'I expect you've already had a full description.'

'You must bring her up here. Show her some children to

coo over.'

'I'll give it some thought.'

She laughed.

Chapter 12
Author: James's Sister

I remember the expression on our mother's face when she returned from that trip to London. 'Jimmy has a girlfriend!'

'What's she like?'

'Oh, she's lovely. Isn't she, Ted?'

'Actually,' my father said, 'she looks a lot like that girl he got pregnant.'

'Margaret Holmes?' I said.

Our mother looked thoughtful. 'I suppose she does. I didn't see that till you pointed it out. Do you suppose he's missing her?'

I knew Margaret was missing him because I'd run into her—or, rather, she'd approached me when I was shopping in Binns.

'It's Jimmy's sister, isn't it?'

'Margaret. How are you?'

She said she was fine, which didn't really square with how she looked. I suggested we go for coffee. At the table she asked politely about me, my husband, my children but that wasn't really where her mind was. 'How is Jimmy?' she asked at last.

'I think he's fine. We don't speak very often, but I get news from my parents. When he gets round to giving them any. He's very busy at the BBC.'

'Yes. I wonder if he ever thinks of me.'

'Well, I should think so, Margaret.' I had no reason to believe any such thing, but what else could I say?

'Or our daughter. I wonder if he thinks about her. Did he tell you I sent him a photo?'

'He didn't, Margaret. No.'

There were tears in her eyes. 'I was obsessed,' she said.

Was?

'I still am,' she said as though she'd read my thoughts.

I held her hand across the table. 'Margaret. You're wearing a wedding ring.'

'Yes. Another mistake. I thought getting married to someone else would stop me thinking about Jimmy. I was wrong.' She spread her arms wide in a sort of shrug. 'I'm sorry. I know how I must look. But...' She wiped away a tear. 'I got pregnant deliberately. I don't suppose Jimmy realised that.'

'No, I don't suppose he did.'

'All I could think of was Jimmy, and how I wanted us to be together always. I thought if I had a baby he'd have to marry me. Happy ever after. What an idiot.'

'I expect your father believed he was doing the right thing by you.' She nodded, without conviction. I said, 'Did you go to Cambridge?'

'Oh, yes. I got my degree. That's where I met the man I'm married to.'

'Do you have children?'

'No! And I'll make sure I never do. Not by him.'

There was really nothing to say to that. Shortly afterwards, we parted. 'Give Jimmy my love next time you speak,' was the last thing she said.

I said I would. Of course, I never did.

When I went through Jimmy's things after his death, the picture of Margaret's baby was there. I'd say from the creased appearance that he looked at it a lot.

Here's some more from IJ. I think it fits here.

As we agreed, I showed the early stages of your brother's book to a gay man of my acquaintance of about the same age and asked how typical this experience was. This is what he says:

"It's different now, because being gay is an accepted choice and people are more understanding, but for a certain kind of young man at that time I think it rings true. We weren't gays to other people; we were 'bumboys' and 'homos' and we were, if we were lucky, looked down on and held in contempt. If we weren't lucky we were viciously beaten up. Homosexuality was illegal and the law was enforced quite rigorously. In fact, he was very lucky that one of those men he picked up, or who

picked him up, wasn't a policeman on the trawl for someone to trap and prosecute. A lot of that went on. It was one of the reasons why we tended to form closed groups; we were always on the lookout for informers.

I say 'a certain kind of young man' because what is clear about your author is that he saw himself as a girl and although I know some people think that's true of gays it usually isn't. This man Ben tried to tell him that and he was right. Although I notice that Ben himself had a thing for boys in girl's underwear, and that isn't the normal gay approach, either. In my experience, most men who dress up as women are probably not looking for same sex partners—they'd be more likely to want a woman who welcomed that fetish. Ben must have thought Christmas had arrived early when your author entered into the spirit of the thing so eagerly.

Where I find the story convincing is in the way it deals with initiation. Just put yourself inside this young man's head for a moment. He knows he's supposed to lust after girls; he knows the feelings he really has are frowned on. He also knows that he can't risk walking up to a man and saying, 'Would you like to go to bed with me?' So what does he do? There's nothing he can do, unless someone else makes the first move. He doesn't have the experience; older men do. But the chances are that no older man will take a chance by approaching him. When Ben did, he saw his opportunity and he took it. Good for him.

He has it right when he says that gay men don't swallow—they usually don't (I'm sorry if that seems like too much information). It's even less likely now, since the arrival of AIDS, but swallowing wasn't normal even then. I also notice that they got up to a lot of anal intercourse and that's something else that was, and is, less common than would appear from this book. Most sex between men is masturbation, fondling, frottage, blow jobs, rimming—we know that an arse that has been buggered too often loses its tightness and a slack arse is a problem we can all live without. However, when I first accepted what I was and allowed a man to break me in I let him bugger me often in the early days because (a) it seemed loving to give myself to him as much as I did; (b) I wasn't aware that I might be storing up problems for the future; and (c) it was

what he wanted, he was bigger and stronger than I was and I would
probably have struggled to prevent him even if I had wanted to. All of
those reasons were probably also factors for your author.

So, if I have to come down on one side or the other, I'd say the story is
probably true as he tells it.

What I think we can say is that his queerness wasn't set in stone, and I
suggest you warn your client that, if she publishes the book, she's going
to face a storm if she doesn't play that down. Gays are no different from
any other group—we expect our view to be the only one that's allowed
and the official gay view is that your sexuality is set from the beginning
and that's that. I've known gay men who might very well have ridden
the other bus had things turned out differently and some who will bed
a woman as fast as they would a man if the chance presents itself,
but we live in a world where orthodoxy is the only faith allowed. We
haven't moved on much since pre-Reformation times, if you want my
opinion. But I can promise you this: your author did not become queer
because of a domineering father or a dominating mother or anything like
that. Some people are dead straight and some are dead queer but most
are somewhere between those extremes. Your author had a lot of the
feminine in him. That's why he was attracted to men. In his youth that
was a sin and a crime and we should all thank God that it is no longer
so.

What's clear when you read his story is that he enjoyed sex with women
but he also enjoyed sex with men and I'm glad he did. Why the hell
shouldn't he? I wish I'd known him at the time. I'd have taken his
cherry with the greatest of pleasure.

Oh—and one other little titbit I kept back when I was giving you part of IJ's report on Ben. This is what he said:

You may like to know that Ben was an only child. Belinda
was a gay woman of his acquaintance, and not his sister.
She's an old lady now and no longer sexually active, but
when I tracked her down she admitted the deception with
pride. 'He was a young man who would probably have made
himself a nuisance to young women, the way young men
tend to do. Ben led him on a different track entirely. What

self-respecting lesbian would have refused to co-operate in that?' There is no suggestion anywhere in your author's book that he ever realised the truth.

Chapter 13
Author: James

I stopped going to Hampstead Heath. When the men I knew called, I excused myself. I stayed away from Bristol. Only the Tuesday nights with Guy continued.

Then they stopped, too.

Helen went on living in the flat she shared with two other girls, but she spent a lot of time at my place. I gave her a key. She brought some of her clothes over and left them there. She looked deadpan at my stuff. 'You have some very sexy knickers here.'

'Yes.'

'You're my size. Shall I wear them?'

'If you like.' I had to admit they looked better on her. She had the bottom to fill them. And I told myself I didn't need them any more.

She came to bed that night in a pair of my baby dolls. They didn't make her submissive, though. It was still her on top.

Life changed. No more hurried couplings on Hampstead Heath and nights in other men's beds. When you're with a woman, your social life is wider than that.

Helen and I went to parties together. We held one in my flat. "Her" friends became "our" friends; we went to the pictures and the theatre with them. People I'd known at school and university came to visit; with girlfriends or, increasingly often, with wives. Helen and I were an item. I met her parents, who lived in Essex and seemed to like me.

I told myself that this was right. Sex with women is good; sex with men is wrong. Nice, but wrong. I was making myself over. Sex between consenting adult men had become legal, but I didn't need it. I was out of that world.

A youth culture was developing at the BBC. We had pop music shows on television and a radio channel that played nothing else. Some very strange people began to be seen in studios, headphones clamped to their heads. There were rumours that weren't really rumours because everyone knew they were true. Girls below the age of consent thronged the places from which some of the strange men broadcast and the strange men exercised *droit de seigneur*. Everyone knew it; nobody did anything to stop it.

Jimmy Savile was the strangest man of all. He'd been a bouncer. He wasn't married; he worshipped his mother; he always had a cigar in his fingers or between his lips; he had staring eyes behind coloured glasses and a collection of catchphrases that suggested he wasn't entirely sane. As a fellow Northerner, I saw him and discounted him—an obnoxious dickhead. In the Home Counties environment of the BBC, he was held in awe. He was the future. He would bring mass young audiences to the BBC. The fact that the BBC was bringing young people *en masse* to the man himself seemed to pass the bosses by. They knew, though. Don't ever believe they didn't. They knew and they didn't care.

I had met Savile a few times and I didn't like him. Then one day, I walked into a rehearsal room that was supposed to be empty and found him in a chair with a girl who wore a pass saying she was a visitor to one of Radio 1's pop music programmes. Radio 1 had taken over from the Light Programme only a year earlier and it was the BBC's programme for young people. Older survivors from the Light Programme were expected to listen to Radio 2. I felt that young people might also be attracted to Radios 3 and 4 but emerging thinking was that this was nonsense—Radio 3 was elitist and should be phased out, while most young people were simply too thick to follow the spoken words uttered on Radio 4. The words "too thick" really belong in quotation marks because they were, indeed, a quotation—not from one of the public school BBC men but from a thirty-year-old female colleague educated at Leeds Grammar School and Cambridge.

The girl was sitting on Savile's knee. Her blouse was open, her brassiere was undone, her knickers were on the floor and his hand was between her legs. When I entered the room I thought the expression in her eyes as she looked at me was one of entreaty. Nevertheless, deeply ingrained habits of Englishness prevailed; I said, 'Oh, I'm sorry,' went out of the room and shut the door.

I leaned with my back against the door and my eyes closed. I couldn't really have seen what I thought I had seen. Surely? What wouldn't go away was that look in the girl's eyes. I wanted to walk away. I knew I couldn't.

A man was passing in the corridor. I grabbed him by the shoulder. 'Come with me. I need a witness.' I threw the door open and stepped inside, pulling my witness with me.

The scene was unchanged. I said to the girl, 'Put your clothes on and come with me.'

She scrambled to her feet and pulled her knickers on, then fastened her brassiere and began to button her blouse. Savile put a cigar between his wet lips and stared at me with amusement. My witness turned on me a look of absolute loathing. 'Why did you bring me in here?'

'I told you. I need a witness.'

'You haven't got one.' As he headed for the door, he said, 'You're out of your mind.'

Savile's amusement had intensified. He didn't say a word.

The girl wanted to know where I was taking her.

'To my office, to call Personnel. They'll know what to do.' Helen was away for the week, visiting her mother who was recovering from a nasty operation. I hadn't been assigned a replacement, so I had to make the phone calls myself. Security were there in minutes and the girl was taken away. I heard no more till the next day; when I arrived at my desk there was a message on it asking me to go to the Personnel Director's office without delay.

The director wasn't there but one of her colleagues was. He asked me to describe the events of the previous day and I did so. What happened next stunned me.

'James, you have given a very full account of what you say

happened. So full, that what I find hard to understand is that there is no supporting evidence at all.'

'I've given you a witness…'

'…who denies having seen anything. Not the girl, not Jimmy Savile, not you.'

'But he…'

'Let me finish. The witness says he was not in that corridor at that time. In fact, he says he was in a meeting on another floor and the person he says he was with confirms his account.'

'But…'

'And Jimmy Savile was not in the rehearsal room you mention. We have not questioned him but the room was reserved by a producer and he has confirmed that he was there. Not Savile. A producer.'

'It's a cover-up.'

'The one confirmation we have been able to obtain is from the guard who collected the girl from your office yesterday. He says she was in a very distressed state and her clothes gave every indication of having been interfered with.'

I could not believe I was being stitched up like this. 'And the girl? What does she say?'

'The girl left without being spoken to. The guard took her to the canteen and bought her a cup of tea and a chocolate éclair while he looked for his supervisor to seek guidance. When he returned, she had gone.'

I stared at him. Not a flicker passed over his face. I said, 'The éclair is a nice touch.'

'I beg your pardon?'

'What was it Gilbert said? "Corroborative detail, intended to give artistic verisimilitude to an otherwise bald and unconvincing narrative."'

'The only things we can be sure of are that there was a girl, she was in your room and when she emerged from it she was distressed and her clothes had been tampered with.'

'I want the girl interviewed. And not by you; I want the

police involved.'

'We can certainly have the girl spoken to, James.' He picked up a pen. 'Give me her name.'

'I don't know it.'

'Aah.' He put the pen down again. 'As for the police, of course you may contact them. If you think that's wise. You might wish to consider what else might come out, and the Press catch wind of. It is not BBC policy to interfere in the private lives of its staff, but that doesn't mean we are not aware of interesting aspects in your own relationships.' He leaned forward, elbows on the desk, hands clasped. 'In any case, in the absence of what you call corroborative detail I'm afraid we must bring your BBC career to an end.'

I felt an almost physical pain, as though my body was about to give way. He said, 'There are two ways we can go. Dismissed for cause, without compensation, and we pass the information we have to the police. Or we can agree to let you go in order to confront the demons you obviously face. In that case we could be generous. Shall we say, a year's salary?'

'I'll tell you what I don't understand,' I said. 'Why is Savile so important? How can he get away with what he does get away with?'

'We're not talking about him, James. We're talking about you. Of course, if the girl comes back and makes a complaint then we would have to involve the police. And I'm sure we could find her if we wanted to.'

I knew when I was beaten. I signed the document he had ready, he gave me a cheque for an amount that in many parts of the country would still at that time buy a nice house, I cleared my desk and went home. My BBC career was over.

Chapter 14
Author: James & Lucy

As I've said, Helen wasn't living with me. She spent a lot of time at my place and kept a lot of things there, but she had kept on her flat share, and when she went to work the following day she went straight from her parents' house in Essex. She rang at six, suggesting we meet for coffee. Not dinner; coffee. The place she named was very close to where she lived, but she didn't ask me to pick her up—she said she'd see me there. She hung up before I could say anything else.

'When were you planning to tell me?'

'When we met. When we talked. Now, I suppose, since I haven't heard from you all day.'

'James. I went to work this morning for the first time in a week. When I got there I learned that the man I worked for had been fired for fornicating with an under-age girl.'

'I did no such thing.'

'It's what people are saying. The man I worked for was also the man who I thought loved me, and he loved me so much he didn't bother to warn me about what I was going to walk into.'

'I'm sorry.'

'You're sorry. I've heard a lot of stuff today, James. You know what the most striking thing has been?'

'Tell me.'

'It's you, in the position you're in, saying you're getting round to talking about it now because you haven't heard from me earlier. *You* haven't heard from *me*. Did it really never cross your mind that I needed to hear about the mess you were in before I got there?'

When she put it that way, I could see her point.

'Are you really so monumentally self-centred, James, that you thought you were the only person affected?'

'I didn't think anything. I wasn't thinking at all. And I'm

sorry. Of course I should have told you. I've been so numb, I haven't thought about anything. I'm sorry.'

'Stop saying you're sorry, Jimmy. It's too late for sorry. I rang you last night. I rang at six and there was no answer and I rang at ten and there was no answer. Where were you?'

'I wasn't answering the phone.'

'You weren't out?'

'No.'

'You didn't have someone else with you?'

'No.'

'You just felt too sorry for yourself to answer the phone when the woman who thought you loved her called?'

'I'm sorry. I didn't know it was you.'

'Jimmy. I've called you every evening I've been away. I've called to tell you about my day and how my mother was doing, she's much better thank you for asking, and to say how I was looking forward to seeing you again. Why would I suddenly not call last night?'

I didn't say anything. I felt beaten down into silence.

'You know what's going on here, James? I'm holding up a mirror. I'm inviting you to look at yourself and see what other people see. I thought you loved me.'

'I do love you.'

'In your terms, maybe. Not in normal people's. I dreamed you were the one; that we'd get married, have children together.'

'So did I. I mean, so do I.'

'No, Jimmy. That dream died today. You may be too weak to think properly but I can be strong enough for both of us. I'm going to your place now to pick up my stuff. It'll take me half an hour and I'd like you to stay away from there for that long. I'll leave my key on the table when I'm done.'

I couldn't believe it was ending like this. I sat and stared at her.

'I'll leave your knickers,' she said. 'You may need them again. When you find a proper man to take care of you.'

I thought at the time that that was the cruellest thing that had ever been said to me. After she walked out, I sat and cried. Other customers walked round me, and eventually the manager asked me to leave.

It's hard to remember how we managed our lives before mobile phones. If these events were happening today, mine would have been buzzing while Helen listed my shortcomings for me. It would ring again as I left the coffee shop, and this time I would answer, and it would be Guy. 'Well,' he'd say. 'Here's another fine mess you've got yourself into.' That would just redouble my unhappiness. I'd stand on the pavement and sob and Guy would say, 'Get into a taxi. Can you manage that?'

But in 1969 we didn't have mobile phones. Instead, Guy had sent a car for me. The driver was waiting patiently. Why wouldn't he? He was being paid. He handed me a note that said, "I'm sorry about the mess you're in. Come and eat. Stay the night if you can. The driver will bring you."

Guy said, 'Look at the state of you.'
'I'm sorry.'
'Oh, you're sorry.' He was imitating me, a high pitched sorry-for-yourself moan, his head wagging from side to side like an Indian's. 'You know, Jimmy, you're a very good advertisement for public schools.'
'I didn't go to one.'
'Exactly. If you had, you'd be a hell of a lot better at managing your feelings. Go and get in the bath. Warm yourself up.'
I did what I was told. In the heat of the water I began to feel a little better. Not a lot; but a little. Guy came in while I was soaping myself. He scooped off the floor the clothes I had just taken off and hung a nightie in burgundy silk over the hook on the door. 'This is yours. Remember it?'

* * *

We ate soup, good and hot, with rye bread. Three different kinds of cheese. More than a bottle of claret. Coffee. A large glass each of Lagavulin with a little water added.

Guy said, 'What will you do now?'

'I don't know. The BBC is the only job I've ever had. I don't know anything else. I suppose I could teach, but...'

'How do you fancy California?'

'Lovely. But what...'

'I have a friend in LA. We were at Oxford together. I think he'd find a place for you. Get you a green card. You could make a new life. Get away from everyone who knows you. Would you like me to contact him?'

'Yes, please.'

Then we went to bed. Guy laid me on my front, folded my nightie under my arms and went to work with Vaseline. Feeling his fingers there brought back everything I'd been missing during my time among the straights. Then he pushed his way into me and had me. I'd never been Lucy for Guy and I didn't introduce the two of them that night, but Lucy is who I was as I lay under him and I was still Lucy when he tossed me off afterwards and, later, when I fell asleep in his arms.

Chapter 15
Author: James & Lucy

House prices had been rising in London and demand was high. I sold my flat within two weeks of putting it on the market and after clearing the mortgage I had a decent sum left over. Add to that the cheque I'd received from the BBC and I had enough to buy a small house a thousand yards from Venice Beach and furnish it.

Guy's friend was called Nick, he ran a news gathering agency and he summed me up fairly quickly. 'You see yourself on the distaff side, I think.'

I made up my mind on the spot. 'The man who initiated me used to call me Lucy.' There. It was out. I was taking a chance and if I'd regret it, I'd regret it.

'Initiated,' he said. 'That's a nice word.'

'It was a nice thing for him to do.'

'You need a bear.'

I didn't know what gay men meant by a bear. I was to find out.

Nick threw a party that weekend. Actually, Nick threw a party most weekends, but the one I'm talking about was a special day for me. 'Wear anything you like,' he said, 'as long as it's casual. But if you have anything feminine to put on under it, do. I'll be introducing you to someone who is particularly turned on by the idea of an English Lucy. I'm expecting to see you leave with him.'

'I'd better not drive to your place, then.'

'Take a cab.'

Nick's house in West Hollywood was hacienda style, finished in pink with a high wall (also pink) all the way round it. I'm sure neighbours knew what kind of men they saw going through the gate, but the wall made sure they couldn't see what those men got up to. Not that I think neighbours in West Hollywood would have cared. Bougainvillea grew over the walls; the pool, which was the biggest I'd ever seen, was surrounded by succulent plants.

Nick's parties were catered. Hispanic waiters stood behind two long tables groaning under salads and meat and seafood that would have enabled any guest—vegan or carnivore; Christian, Jewish or Moslem—to satisfy himself. A barman tended a third table. Nick took a daiquiri from him and handed it to me, then led me to a group of five men who all eyed me with undisguised interest. 'Guys,' he said. 'This is Lucy.' The interest visibly increased. He introduced them to me but I had little hope of remembering the names first time around.

I did, however, know the name of the man who separated me from the group because how could I not when I had seen him so many times on cinema screens? Although, as I would discover, the name I knew him by—Marty Bone—was not the one his German immigrant parents had given him when he had been born in Brooklyn forty years earlier. Marty played heroic leading man roles; the all-American male who led the good guys to victory against overwhelming odds and always got the girl in the last reel. He was a film producer's wet dream: six feet something in height; blue eyes; blond hair with the hint of a wave to it; forearms my hands would not go round and biceps more than twice as thick as that; a huge chest from which more blond hair curled over the collar of his tight shirt; a flat stomach. This, I realised, was a bear. And not just any bear—this was the bear who wanted to meet the English Lucy.

He was shepherding me away from the others. Herding me as a dog herds sheep. I would have been annoyed had I not been so utterly turned on. I knew people were watching, knew they were amused and I didn't care. I had a feeling of being among friends.

The thought that comes to me now is: Where was Helen in all of this? Had I completely forgotten her? When she dumped me I had cried tears that had seemed endless; had they been for nothing? And the answer, I know, is that I had loved Helen and I'd wanted and expected to marry her and if we had done so my life would have unfolded in a completely different way. But we hadn't and we weren't going to; and now I was in a different country, physically as well as figuratively, and I was loving the endless sunshine and the sense of boundless possibilities and the freedom to be whatever you wanted to be. Helen had left me. Okay; so I would find someone else. And here, in the shape of Marty, was a very attractive candidate.

Marty guided me through an arch into the house. He knew where he was going and I didn't doubt he had done this in this house before. We went through an immense kitchen in which another Hispanic man was working, across a wide hallway and up a flight of stairs to a landing. In front of us was a series of doors.

'You've never been here,' said Marty, 'so I'll explain the convention. At the start, Nick leaves a key on the outside of each of these doors. When you go into a bedroom, take the key out and lock the door on the inside. Or don't bother to lock it; no-one is going to open a door that doesn't have a key in it. That would be the worst possible manners and our host detests bad manners.'

It was early in the day's partying but already more keys were out of the doors than in them. Even in such a big house with so many bedrooms, there must have been times when people had to line up and wait to fornicate. But two doors had keys on show and Marty removed one of them from the lock, opened the door, stood back, said, 'After you, Lucy,' followed me into the room and locked the door behind us. He took the untasted daiquiri out of my hand and placed it on a dressing table.

We were in a large, light and airy bedroom in the centre of which was a bed bigger than any I had seen till then. On each side of the bed were tables and on each of the tables were the bottle of lotion and the tissues I had become used to seeing in queers' bedrooms together with a blue tube, which I had not. I just had time to look at one of the tubes and see that it was made by Johnson & Johnson before Marty picked me up as though I had no weight at all and threw me, on my back, onto the middle of the bed.

He followed me. It was a high bed, but he seemed just to vault onto it. He came down on top of me, pinning me, but without hostile intent because he propped his head on a hand and smiled down at me. Then he kissed me. He kissed me on the lips, on the forehead, on the cheek, on the other cheek, on the throat and on the lips again. My hands rested on his huge upper arms and I kissed him back.

He sat up next to me, undid my belt, unbuttoned the loose shorts I was wearing and pulled them down. Underneath I was wearing grey silk panties, loose in the leg. He put his hand gently on the front, feeling my strengthening cock. 'Oh, my, Lucy,' he said. He unbuttoned my shirt and found the grey silk camisole that matched the panties. 'Oh, my, oh, my. You sexy chick. Come on.' He slipped the panties down to my knees, gave the palm of his hand a good squirt of lotion from one of the bottles and wrapped it around me. I threw both arms round his neck and hugged him close, smothering his face with kisses as he masturbated me. I had no restraint and no staying power and he had to grab for the tissues as I came more suddenly than I had since I was a boy playing with myself before Ben came into my life. I kept hugging him. I could see the point of bears.

He said, 'I'd love to stay here with you all day, honey, but I have some business to transact with the guys downstairs. I want to know that you're mine. Party, have a good time, enjoy yourself but when you leave you leave with me. Deal?'

I nodded. 'Deal.' How could he possibly imagine I'd go with someone else when I could have him?

He said, 'There's just time for a quickie.' He lay back on the bed, unzipped his linen slacks and took the back of my head in his hand. What he wanted was obvious and it was no problem to me. I knelt, taking over the job of unveiling no ordinary penis but an uncoiling and rampant weapon. It was huge—bigger than any I had ever seen—so big that I could scarcely get the tip into my mouth.

'You like that?' he gasped as my tongue slithered over his

slit.

I couldn't speak; I managed to grunt an affirmation.

'That's a good girl,' he said. 'Don't speak with your mouth full. Your mother brought you up right. You'd better like it, sweetheart, because it's going up your ass tonight. All of it. All the way.'

If I'd been able to think, that might have given me pause, but thinking was beyond me. I washed that monstrous tool with my tongue and all the love I could bring to bear, and when I felt the sudden contractions that said he was about to come I clamped my mouth firmly in place and took his whole load into it. Then I sat back and swallowed. Whatever Ben said, I was a swallower. If that meant I wasn't really gay, so be it. Lying on that beautiful bed in that room filled with warm sunshine, I liked the way I was. However you defined it. I grinned at Marty. He smiled back.

'Till tonight,' I said.

He threw his arms round me and hugged me so tight I felt as though my ribs might break.

'Till tonight,' he said.

I picked up my glass and took my first ever sip of daiquiri. Like everything else in California, I loved it.

Chapter 16
Author: James's Sister

As Jimmy wrote this book, Chapter 15 doesn't end there. I've interrupted because I want to say a couple of things.

First, Jimmy says, 'I had loved Helen and I'd wanted and expected to marry her and if we had done so my life would have unfolded in a completely different way.' I'm sorry but I just don't think that's true. I'm not saying he was lying—I don't think that, consciously, he was—but he was seeing himself as, really, he wasn't. What I think Jimmy was in love with was not Helen; it was the idea of being "normal." Any gay man or woman today would be outraged by that expression, but that's how it looked in the Sixties. There were just as many people like Jimmy then as there are now but they mostly kept it to themselves and satisfied their desires in private. The face the public saw was the face of the married person with children. That passed for "normal" then. And when he says, "If that meant I wasn't really gay, so be it," he's closer to the truth than he knows. Jimmy wasn't in his heart of hearts gay or straight. Jimmy was whatever gave him most pleasure at the time. If he leaned towards gayness it was because he could be "the girl" and expect a strong man to take care of things for him. Today, no woman with any sense would accept that kind of relationship with a man because she'd know she could be let down just when it would do most damage, but in those days that's how it was. When he was in a relationship with a woman—Helen, for example—she expected him to behave like an adult and he didn't want to do that at that time. He changed. As you will see. But right then, he was what he was.

Which brings us to the second thing I want to say, because even as I write "there were just as many people like Jimmy" I realise that it's nonsense—there was almost no-one like Jimmy then and there still isn't. I think he did eventually grow up, but he hadn't in his mid to late twenties which is the time he was writing about here. Just watch him cavorting with "Marty Bone". He's wearing silk panties and a camisole and he's behaving like a child. A young girl child if we want to be exact. You wouldn't be surprised to see him skipping around the yard flicking up the edges of his skirt. My cousin has a lovely daughter who I see from time to time. She's fourteen now, she's bright and doing well at school and I expect one day to see her in a worthwhile career but above all else she's bubbly and giggling. She likes boys, as long as they're nice to her, but I don't think there's anything sexual in it—not yet. Of course, I could be wrong and it's possible that behind the open face is a mind seething with lust, but so far as I can tell she sees life as a big party laid on by a kind universe for us all to enjoy and she takes what Fate sends. When I look at her, I see the young Jimmy, and the joy he took just from being in California.

Okay; that's what I wanted to say. Except that Jimmy's trouble with the BBC over Jimmy Savile came as a complete surprise because my parents and I knew nothing about it. Until I read this book, I believed what he told us at the time—that his BBC career was fine but he'd been offered a job in America and couldn't resist the challenge. We'll carry on now, but we'll give it a new chapter. Before we do, I suppose I'd better mention Marty. I don't know how obvious his real identity is to a casual reader—I've changed his name as I've changed everyone's, including Jimmy's, but there weren't many Marty Bone lookalikes around. He's dead now, so he isn't going to sue, but he was a good friend as well as a sex partner for Jimmy and I don't want to hurt him even in memory.

Chapter 17
Author: James & Lucy

That was the first of Nick's parties I'd been to, and I loved it. I was the centre of attention, but Marty had staked a claim and you didn't jump one of Marty's claims. I had a few cuddles, a few kisses; my backside was felt and from time to time a hand brushed the front of my shorts but I knew I was leaving with Marty and so did everyone else.

When the time came, I was ready. I've never been a car person but I know Marty's car was a Shelby KR500 convertible because Marty told me. Several times. He also told me it had a Cobra jet engine and that it was the most powerful Mustang ever built, which meant that it was really a Ford. All of this went over my head. What I was aware of was that I was with one of the most charismatic movie stars ever, that I was sitting on something he wanted, and that I intended to give it to him as soon as politeness allowed. One time when Helen and I were on the Tube on our way to my place she said, 'I've got a wet spot and it's getting bigger by the second.' I couldn't do her kind of wet spot because I didn't have that sort of lubrication but I swear she felt no hornier than I did that day in the Shelby.

What struck me first about Marty's home was its ordinariness. Ordinary, that is, by Malibu standards. Where I grew up it would have been regarded as stunning. These houses had a pattern and the pattern was one of privacy. The master bedroom, which was where we went first, was big enough to throw a party of maybe thirty people. One wall was almost all glass, the centre a sliding door about twelve feet wide which opened onto a patio; beyond the patio was a garden with lawn, shrubs, a pond and flower beds. There were blinds on the windows but Marty didn't bother to close them because the garden was surrounded by an impenetrable hedge twelve feet high and, when the help wasn't there (and it wasn't there on the evening I'm talking about), no-one would be able to see in. The four poster bed was square, immense and covered in cushions. At the foot of the bed was a sofa wide enough for four people. On a table beside the bed were the accoutrements I had come to expect.

Marty ran one huge arm around half of the cushions and threw them to the floor. He went to the other side and repeated this action with the other half. He heaved the bedspread onto the floor and pulled down the top sheet. Then he sat on the sofa. 'The shirt and the shorts,' he said.

I pretended not to know exactly what he meant. 'What about them?'

'We don't need them.'

I stood in front of him and did a striptease. When I was down to my grey silk panties and camisole he held out his enormous paws. I put my hands in them and he pulled, gently but irresistibly, until I fell into his lap. He wrapped his great arms round me. I let myself be enfolded. I kissed him on the lips. Then came the same exchange I'd once had with Guy.

'Anything you don't do?'

'I haven't found it yet.'

He stood up, not seeming to notice my weight as I hung by my arms around his neck. He laid me on the bed, more gently than when he'd thrown me there earlier at Nick's house. After our session there I was expecting to be ravished, but either he was more considerate than I expected or the blow job I had given him earlier had made him patient. I lay on my back watching him undress and wondering how, exactly, I was going to take that monstrous pole without suffering damage. When he was naked, he lay beside me. His hand began to stroke my thigh. 'Do you shave your legs?'

'The first man I lived with, the first who had me in fact, his sister showed me how to do it. So I could wear stockings.'

His hand had left my thigh and slipped beneath the leg of my panties. 'Not much call for stockings in this climate.' He cupped my balls tenderly. 'If you wear dresses, though?'

'I do when nobody can see me.'

'Nobody?' Now his fingers were stroking that magical, sensitive place between balls and bottom.

'Nobody I don't want to see me.'

He withdrew his hand, sat up and slipped my panties down: to my knees; to my ankles; off. I let my legs part. He said, 'I'd like to see you in a dress.'

'I'd like you to.'

He lifted my camisole and I raised my shoulders so that he could get it off me. He stroked my chest. 'You're in good shape,' he said. 'You should stay that way.'

'I'll do my best.'

'Be careful about what you eat. Don't drink alcohol more than three days a week. And join a gym.'

'A gym?' Gyms in England at that time were rough places that smelled of sweat and liniment. Or so I understood.

'I'll take you to the one I go to. The guy who owns it, he's an ex-boxer and he's only interested in girls so when you're there you're straight. But you'll thank me.' He reached over to the bedside table for the ubiquitous bottle of lotion and squirted some into his hand. I wrapped my arms as far round his back as I could get them while, slowly and tenderly and with many kisses, he stroked me till I came. We lay in each other's arms. He seemed in no hurry to go further. He kissed me. He stroked me. He kissed me again.

Then he took my hand and placed it on him. He wasn't completely hard yet, but still it was huge. 'So,' he said. 'What do you think?'

'I think you'd better go slowly.'

'But you can take it?'

'I'm certainly going to try.'

'If it gets too much, tell me.'

'Okay.'

'Turn onto your front for me, honey.'

I did. He took my arms and put them over my head. He sat beside me and stroked my back, all the way down to the bottom. Then his lips replaced his hands. Starting at my neck, he began to kiss, lick and nibble all the way from there to the base of my spine. As he got closer to the bottom, his hands pressed my buttocks apart and his thumbs and fingers began to stroke the inside slopes, closer and closer to the centre. I'd never had this. Men had had me there, and I'd enjoyed it, but no-one had ever paid this amount of loving attention to the hole they were about to push themselves into. If I knew nothing else, I knew now that my pleasure was as important to Marty as his own.

His mouth grew ever closer and the pressure pushing my buttocks apart increased. I was wide open to him. And then his tongue was pushing in, sliding over the places his fingers had caressed, pushing, pushing...and it was there. The tip of his tongue played on my hole. I squirmed in delight.

'You okay?' asked Marty.

'Oh, God. Oh, God. That is so wonderful.'

'You've never been rimmed before?'

'Never!'

'You like it?'

'I *love* it.'

I've written that as though it had been an ordinary conversation. In fact, I was convulsed, and gasping so much I could hardly get the words out. His tongue pressed on, and in, and as it pressed I felt myself opening before it. I would never have believed this, but the tip of his tongue was now inside my anal passage, and I was in heaven. And this was rimming; this was the activity that Ben did not like and would not do. *Why?* I would never understand.

At last, and just when I thought I would reach my climax from being rimmed alone, Marty withdrew his tongue. He reached over to the table and picked up the blue tube. I said, 'What *is* that?'

'K-Y Jelly. They still using Vaseline in England?' He had taken the top off the tube and was squeezing it directly into my hole. My cock was utterly rigid.

'That's all I've ever seen there.'

'This is better.'

His fingers were thicker than some penises I had seen. (Actually, as I write that I know it isn't true. I'm exaggerating for effect. I've never really seen a penis that wasn't at least as thick as the thickest of his fingers. But they were thick. And one of them had pushed its way inside me and was spreading the gel there).

'We need to get your love canal lubed up,' he said as he withdrew his finger and squeezed in more gel before returning to the task. When he felt he'd applied enough he put the tube down and began to get serious with his fingers. First one, then two, then—although I'd have said I could not accommodate another—three were inside me together. They twisted, they turned, they spread out; and what he called my love canal spread with them. All the time he was doing this he kept his body pressed tight against mine and kissed me—on the back of the neck; on the cheek—and when he stopped kissing it was to nibble my earlobes.

It was too much. I shot my load into the rich Egyptian cotton sheets. In the moment of utter relaxation that follows ejaculation, Marty seized his chance. Before he came to rest he had more than an inch inside me. And now I knew it was going to be all right. If I had that much in me I could take the rest.

Marty turned me onto my side. He was lying behind me, very close, his arms wrapped round me, his hands stroking first my stomach and then my hip and then my buttock and then back to my stomach again, on and on, pressing firmly with his palm and letting his fingers play on the skin. And, every so often, he'd advance his claim. Half inch by half inch, he was taking possession of me. It must have been more than fifteen minutes before at last I felt his hip against mine and knew that he was all the way in. In all that time he had not lost a scintilla of hardness.

'How do you feel, babe?'

'Filled. Possessed. Owned.'

'It doesn't hurt too much?'

'I can handle it.'

'I'm going to start moving, honey. If you need me to stop, say so. Right?'

'Marty. This is what I came here for. Do it.'

As he rolled me onto my front he kissed me once more on the back of the neck. His knees were between mine and he separated them to spread my legs further. He began to move. He'd emptied himself into my mouth earlier and now he could go on for a long time—and that's exactly what he did. At first I was aware of him holding back, being gentle, not wanting to hurt me but as he went on the imperative of the penis in motion took over. It was hard. It was fast. And I loved it. When he came it felt as though I was being given an enema.

He lay on top of me. I couldn't have moved if I'd wanted to. Fortunately, I didn't want to. In the end it was Marty who moved. He lay beside me and stroked my back. 'How do you feel, kiddo?'

'Reamed,' I said.

'Yeah, I opened you up all right. Think you can move?'

'Do I have to?'

'Well, just lie still a minute.' He went away and when he came back he was carrying the warm wet cloth, like a face cloth, that I was becoming used to, and a towel. He cleaned me. 'There's no blood,' he said.

'Good.' I murmured the word; I was drowsy and ready for sleep.

'You may walk a bit awkwardly for a while.'

'Yes.'

'You sorry we did it?'

Was he crazy? I asked the question. 'Are you crazy?'

'Just wanted to know, kid.'

'Are *you* sorry?'

'Not me. That was one of the best times in my life. But I'm not the one whose just been ploughed open.'

Chapter 18
Author: James

Marty did take me to his gym and, after a few weeks, I was as glad to be going there as he had said I would be. Gyms then weren't like they are now, with Nautilus machines and personal trainers. This gym was there to train boxers. Walter, the ex-boxer who owned it, was prepared to accept a small number of non-fighting members so long as they were famous and boosted his gym's reputation by their presence. I wasn't famous, but Walter let me join because Marty asked him to and they didn't come much more famous than Marty.

Walter didn't like faggots. That's the word he used and he spat when he said it. I'd have walked away but the gym was important to Marty and what mattered to Marty mattered to me. I stopped shaving my legs.

In three months I put on twelve pounds, all of it in the biceps, the thighs and the shoulders. I wished Ben could see me now. I wasn't so slight any more. Walter, although he couldn't seem to stop laughing about it, taught me how to punch and how to stop other people punching me. I'd never have made a boxer and he told me so, but I was a lot more confident now about handling myself in general population. General population was an expression you heard quite often at Walter's gym—he may not have admitted faggots or nobodies but ex-cons were welcome.

Something else Walter talked to me about was diet, and I took his advice. He was way ahead of his time on high protein, low carbs. 'And stay off the alcohol, kid. It may gave you a buzz but it's empty calories and it's sugar.' I was twenty-six now, but to Walter I was still "Kid". And not in the sense of Kid Carlton, star of the ring. Not *that* ring, anyway, as Marty put it.

On the Monday after that first party, which I had left to go to Marty's place with the intention of being buggered, Nick came into the room he had given me as an office. 'Everything go okay with Marty, Jimmy?'

I probably blushed. 'Yes, Nick. Fine.'

'One hears things about Marty's size.'

'They're not exaggerated. But I'm walking okay again now.'

He smiled. 'Listen. If you want, you can tell me this is not my business. But I won't be happy with myself unless I say it. Marty's affairs have an arc. They last about six months. Then he needs something new. Some*one* new.'

I nodded. 'Okay.'

'It's natural to think you may be the one that changes the pattern. The true love he settles down with. And you may be, of course.'

'But don't count on it?'

'That would be my advice.'

'Thanks for telling me.'

'It never ends badly. There's always a gift at the end.'

'What? Like setting up the pensioned-off tart in a flat in Limehouse?'

'Much more creative than that. You'll see.'

And it was. As we got closer to the six month mark, I began to see signs that I would not be the one who changed Marty's pattern—the one he settled down with. I didn't mind. That time with Marty was great, it got me into parties with people I wouldn't have met otherwise, but Marty was no more the great love of my life than I was of his. There were people I saw on the streets of Venice who I'd have liked to get to know. It's an interesting place, Venice—I sometimes thought that more of America's loonies lived there than anywhere else on the continent. There was a vibe to the place, a buzz, that you didn't get elsewhere. It's the same today, except that perhaps a smaller percentage of the population now is differently sane. The difference is that then Marty took so much of my time there was none left for other people and today I can hang out with anyone I like.

Almost from our first days together, Marty had told me I should be an actor. I treated it as the kind of thing people say and I took no notice, but as time went on he said it more often. 'We should get you a screen test.'

'Marty. I've never been to acting school. Never been in a play.'

'Neither had I.'

'Oh. I didn't know that. Anyway, you need a union card. I don't have one.'

'Neither did I. If the right person wants you in, getting a card isn't a problem.'

He arranged the screen test. Lots of people did screen tests who weren't actors and were never going to be. It was part of living in LA. Like going to the Tower if you lived in London. I didn't take it seriously. And then, as we approached the end of our relationship (although I hadn't quite taken that on board yet), he said, 'Better shave your legs, Jimmy.'

'Oh? Why?'

'You're on the casting couch next weekend.' He was nuzzling my throat; he'd already got my shirt off and stroked my chest and now he had one hand inside my unzipped jeans and was gently fingering me.

I said, 'I think you'd better slow down and tell me the story from the beginning.'

'Oscar wants to spend some time with you.'

Oscar. I'd met Oscar. Actually, that isn't true; you couldn't call what we had done "meeting". I'd shaken his hand two or three times in reception lines when his studio was giving a party after a premiere. He'd always looked glazed, as though he didn't know who I or any of the other guests were, or what we were doing there. Another "always" thing about Oscar was that he always had his wife with him. Not a trophy model; Susannah had married Oscar when they were both nineteen and that was fifty years ago and a lot of people said Oscar's success in picking stars was down to Susu's guidance.

Marty had me out of my jeans now. 'Shall we continue this in the bedroom?'

When we reached there, Marty's attentions were as tender as ever but what he was telling me said that it was all coming to an end between us, just as Nick had predicted, and this was my payoff. 'Susu thinks you'll make a fabulous second leading man in Oscar's new TV series.'

'You can't have two leading men.'

'Supporting actor, then.'

'Playing what?'

'This is American television and you're English, so there isn't a lot of choice. You can be the Limey faggot or you can be the treacherous bastard who makes everything go wrong for the American hero.'

'I'd rather be the bastard. I can do bastard. But I can't act and I already have a job.'

'You're acting all the time. Your whole life is an act.'

I stared at him. I'd thought he liked me. 'Don't look at me like that, Jimmy. I'm paying you a compliment, for God's sake. Roll over and let me have that gorgeous butt one last time.'

When things quietened down, we got back to the obstacle of my job with Nick, which Marty said was no obstacle at all. 'Jimmy, do your stuff with Oscar next weekend and you'll be contracted for a twelve part series at a hundred grand a pop. That's one point two million bucks. About what I get for a movie. How long will it take you to earn that kind of money with Nick?'

It was a rhetorical question; if he had wanted an answer it would have been twenty four years. My salary with Nick was fifty thousand dollars a year, which was one and a half times the average household income in America at that time. Marty was talking about my earning for each episode what Nick paid me for two years work.

'So,' I said. 'Tell me about this casting couch.'

'Oscar's seen your test. So he knows you can act. You've got to act again. All weekend. Because you're no longer that man you used to be, are you? But you have to pretend.'

He was speaking in riddles. I said, 'What man am I not?'

'The one whose really a young girl and likes to dress up as one and submit.'

Ah. Yes. Okay.

'You don't even bother with the panties any more. Do you?'

'Not often, no.'

'Lucy has left the building. Is it the gym, do you think?'

Was it? I wasn't sure.

'Do you want to know what I think?'

'Sure. Tell me.'

'I do think it's the gym. You used to have this thing about being protected. I've never met your father but my guess is he treated your sister like a pet to be cossetted and looked after and he expected you to be able to look after yourself. You liked what she had more than what you had, and now you don't.'

'My father made me gay? I don't think I'm buying that.'

'I'm not saying your father made you gay. But you're not gay, are you? Not really.'

'You just fucked me up the arse.'

'Ass, Jimmy. You're in America now. Yes, I did. And you enjoyed it. But you'd have enjoyed it as much if you'd been doing the fucking. And if it had been a woman. I fuck women sometimes because I have to. I don't enjoy it. You'd fuck anyone, man or woman, because what you enjoy is the sex itself. You recognise yourself here?'

I did recognise myself. I wasn't sure I wanted to say so, though.

'You're going to spend next weekend with Oscar,' said Marty. 'I know people think Oscar doesn't notice anybody but, believe me, he does. He's noticed you. And he's heard about Lucy.'

'From you?'

'Never mind who from. He's heard about her. He wants to

spend a weekend at the place he calls his hunting lodge, which is a bit like Versailles-in-the-woods, and he wants to spend it with a playful young woman who, when he gets the panties off her, turns out to have a dick and has enough at stake to keep her trap shut afterwards. You.'

'I didn't even know Oscar liked men.'

'It's one of the better kept secrets. Now you know why he and Susu have stayed married for nearly fifty years. You don't divorce your wife for another man.'

'What about her? What does she want?'

'She likes the same thing he does. Young men in bed. It wouldn't surprise me totally if she wanted to take you to the hunting lodge herself, some other weekend. So, anyways, we have to get you some high class ladies' wear before the weekend. And when you're in it, you have to give the performance of your life as a sweet young babycakes buckling at the knees out of lust for Oscar. Think you can do that? And then you really can say goodbye to Lucy.'

'We still haven't talked about Nick.'

'Nick took you on as a favour for some Limey fag he got laid by twenty years ago. He doesn't need you and he pays you more than you're worth to him. He'll let you go.'

I spent some time thinking about Marty's diagnosis of what looked like being Lucy's last days and I decided he was right, but only partly. The fact is: people change. I had been eighteen when Ben seduced me; now I was twenty-eight. At eighteen I was a shy young man who discovered that pretending to be someone completely other was a defensive shield between him and a world that didn't care one way or the other. It also got me physically and demonstratively loved. Ten years during which—except for the calamitous run-in with Jimmy Savile—everything I'd done had been a success had made defence less necessary. Someone was peeping out from behind the mask. I hoped we'd come face to face one day, because I thought the someone was probably me.

(Pretending to be someone completely other. If that wasn't acting, what was? Marty had a point).

But a weekend with Oscar was going to come before I could move on to the next stage in my life.

The young woman who visited me worked as a dresser at Oscar's studio. She made me strip down to my Calvin Kleins (and I could see her noticing how tight they were), measured me in every conceivable place and direction, got back in her car and drove off. Two days later she was back, this time with enough dresses, skirts, tops, nightwear and lingerie to need five trips back and forth between her car and my bedroom before everything was inside.

She said I'd need to take all my clothes off this time. When I did, she picked up a pair of silk panties. Then she said, 'That's no good.'

'What?'

'How can you try these on when you're carrying that stiffie? Goddamn men.' She knelt in front of me. She sucked expertly, lapping the head with her tongue. When I felt the onrush I put my hands on her head and held her firmly in place until I'd filled her mouth with my seed. She sat back on her heels and smiled. It was a beautiful smile, full of heart and completely meant. A smile that said, "I really enjoyed that." She said, 'Now go to the bathroom and sponge yourself clean. We don't want man-smears on these beautiful panties.'

The dresser's name was Karen and she was there again on Friday afternoon to shave my legs and supervise my preparations. Oscar sent a car and when I got into the back seat in my grey shirtwaister she told me I looked like an angel. 'Oscar's going to love you, baby.' Under the dress everything except the nylons was silk. Silk French knickers. Silk chemise with padded bra. Silk garter belt. The driver loaded two suitcases into the trunk and I wondered how I was supposed to get through that many clothes in two days. Karen took the front passenger seat. I hadn't realised she was coming with me.

'I'll be in the servants' quarters,' she said. 'You'll only see me when you need me.'

The driver, a tall woman with close-cropped grey hair and no tits to speak of, chatted to Karen all the way there. She didn't say a word to me. She must have done this before, she must have known what was going on, but what she thought about it I have no idea. Occasionally Karen would turn in her seat, smile at me and slide her hand under the hem of my dress and up my thigh. When she saw how turned on I was, she blew me a kiss. She said, 'It'll be over before you know it, honey.'

Versailles-in-the-Woods was a hunting lodge from which, so far as I could tell, no-one ever hunted. Oscar told me over dinner (hare, silver mullet, lobster and beef, none of which looked like itself but all of which tasted delicious; the chef who of course was French came to the table as we ate the beef to receive our thanks) that it had been built as a film set for a pioneer movie set in the time of the Indian wars. It was a fort surrounded by a high wooden palisade which gave it such privacy that he had kept it on. It was private, all right. No doubt about that. And just as well, considering what Oscar used it for.

The meal ended with coffee and brandy. Then the fun started. Oscar wanted to chase me round the room but he had a full stomach and dodgy legs and I had to do my running slowly and let him catch me very quickly. He was panting hard when he led me by the hand to a long low sofa and pushed me down into it.

'Lift your skirt for me, baby.'

I slid it up my thighs a little at a time. I was giving a performance; my heart wasn't in this at all but I don't think Oscar could see that. What I had once done because my teenage heart longed for it I did now in my late twenties to win a contract. Looking back, that was when Jimmy Carlton the actor took over whatever part of my life he didn't already control. He was never to relinquish it. And, though I hadn't yet really taken it on board, Jimmy Carlton the actor would turn out to be straight.

'Oh, Jeez, baby.' His hand as it slid into the leg of my French knickers and cupped my balls was gentle. 'Let me show you the bedroom.'

It was the most ornate room I have ever seen. I've travelled in Arabia since then and I've seen furnishings as over the top as it's possible to imagine—silks, gold brocades, tassles, swagged curtain over swagged curtain over swagged curtain, polished wood furniture almost invisible beneath *objets* leafed in gold and set with jewels. The master bedroom in that hunting lodge exceeded in ostentatious vulgarity every single one of them. I could hear my mother's voice: "Oh! The cleaning!"

Oscar sat in a plush velour chair with arms covered in gold leaf and set with lapis lazuli. 'Strip for me, baby.' He was one of the most powerful men Hollywood had ever known, but all I could see was weariness. That was the first time I was ever fully conscious of the gap between the young, full of life and energy and promise, and the old for whom it will all soon be over. I feel it the other way now, but then *I* was the young man with so much to give. I knew I'd never do this again for a man; I also knew that the prize was more than a million dollars and for money like that I was going to put on a show to end all shows.

Karen had told me that dress cost two thousand dollars. I cast it off and threw it into the corner like a used duster. I took the hem of the chemise in both hands; slowly turning, raising it bit by bit and then throwing it after the dress. I ran my hands down my sides and slipped them inside the French knickers. Oscar's breathing was heavy, laborious; his mouth hung open; his eyes were popping. When I got the knickers down to my ankles I slipped them off and threw them into his lap. He grabbed them and held them to his face.

I never did master the art of walking in heels. I stepped out of them where I stood and began to dance towards him, one step at a time. His face was turned up to me; his eyes glistened, wet and rheumy. I could see the bulge in his pants. My striptease had got to him.

Within touching distance, I stopped. He reached out and drew me towards him. He kissed my half-erect penis, taking it wetly into his mouth. 'Oh, baby,' he whispered. He started to pull himself out of the chair. He was halfway up when I saw the change in him. It started with a look of astonishment, a sort of "What? Me? Now? But…" His rise from the chair halted, and then reversed. Back he went, down into his seating position but he didn't stop there; he went on sliding, onto his back, and then from the chair to the floor. There wasn't any doubt. I'd never seen a dead person before but, still, there wasn't any doubt.

What happened next astonished and appalled me because I was alone with Oscar's dead body for no more than twenty seconds and then this baroque bedroom was filled with people. Oscar's personal physician travelled everywhere with him, just as his French chef did. The chef wasn't in the room but the doctor was. A man I'd never seen who turned out to be Oscar's Head of Security was there; he took charge of the rest of us while the doctor was examining Oscar and shaking his head. Karen was there. The driver was there. It took longer, but Susu also came.

Karen put her arms round me. 'Poor baby. Was it a terrible shock?'

I said, 'Were you *watching* us?'

'Watching? We were filming you. Oscar likes to have evidence. In case one of his stars gets ideas of blackmail.'

'Oh, my God.'

The doctor had taken Susu to one side and was speaking quietly to her. There wasn't much doubt about the message. I have to say that, for a woman being told her husband of nearly fifty years was dead, she seemed entirely untroubled.

The security man spoke to Karen but he was pointing at me. 'Get him dressed in something normal and get him out of here. We'll have to call the cops and the coroner and I want him gone before anyone turns up.' He turned to the driver. 'Get everything he brought with him into the trunk. Everything. I don't want a trace of this evening left here. And be quick. If the cops think we've delayed calling them, there'll be questions we won't want to answer. Susu, could you please get hold of the housekeeper?' He pointed at me again. 'We need every dish, every glass, every piece of cutlery he might have touched washed and put away, and the same for these two,' at which he pointed at Karen and the driver, 'and everything else left.'

'It's too late,' said Susu. 'Every single thing will be in the dishwashers already.'

'Okay. Good. But let's get three of each out of there and put away so there's no suggestion of any extra guests who've left before the cops get here.' He looked at me. 'Look, bud, I know you've had a shock but standing there like a fucking statue, sorry Susu, isn't going to help anyone. Get dressed as if you were a man and get out of here.' Then to the driver again, 'The Police will come from the south, so you leave to the east. I know it'll make the journey longer but I don't want them seeing you and wondering where you've been.'

This time, Karen sat in the back with me. 'You were very good,' she said. 'You put on a hell of a performance.'

'All wasted now.'

'No! Why?'

'Well, he's dead.'

'Baby, it was never Oscar who was going to make the decision. Not on his own. And Susu was impressed.'

The driver sniggered. 'She was when she saw the size of his cock.'

'Yeah. Listen, Jimmy, do you only swing the one way?'

'No, I bloody well don't.'

'No, I bloody well don't. God, I love that English accent.'

'As a matter of fact, I prefer it with women.'

'Always?'

'Always now. Not when I was young. But now I'm straight. By preference.'

'Well. Good. You were going to let Oscar fuck you so you could get into the movies.'

'You make me sound like a tart.'

'Listen, lots of women have got there the same way. And now I'm sorry but you're probably also going to have to do it with Susu. She's old and wrinkled, but so was Oscar, so just think about the money and make sure you get it up and keep it up.'

'What kind of movies am I being auditioned for?'

'Not porno, if that's what you're afraid of. Susu will want to feel she has a hold on you and she only knows one way to do that.'

Karen stayed with me that night. We went to bed together; we made love; I took the lead. That's what she wanted. For a woman who lived among the kind of people she did, she was amazingly meat-and-potatoes about sex. She made it look as though she had stayed to comfort me after the shock I'd endured, and maybe that was true, but she enjoyed the sex for its own sake. And so did I.

Next day she told me to stay home while she went to see Susu. When she came back, she brought a contract for me to sign. 'This is it, babe. The start of your movie career. Susu says you have to stay away until after the funeral, but then she wants you in her bed. The contract is good, but if you don't come across she'll find a way to break it. Okay? Okay, Jimmy?'

'Okay, Karen. No problem.'

'You want me to stay again tonight?'

'What do you want to do?'

'I'd like to stay. But if you want me to go I'll go, no hard feelings.'

'I'd like you to stay.'

We spent most of the afternoon walking on the beach and the boardwalk. That evening we ate out. Most of my neighbours had never seen me with a woman and that evening I got smiles and waves warmer than anything I'd seen before.

Chapter 19
Author: James's Sister

Do you read Hollywood memoirs? *The Elephant to Hollywood,* for example (that was Michael Caine, in case you haven't, and the Elephant in question is the Elephant and Castle). Shirley MacLaine—*My Lucky Stars?* Actually, that one isn't bad—she does what most film stars won't do and lets you see some big names in unflattering terms. But the usual run, and I do include the Michael Caine book in this, is a series of names of films. some memorable and some , larded with stories about "my very good friend so-and-so" and "my very good friends him and her" with no suggestion that anyone in the movie business might be less than a perfect person.

And that, frankly, is not how it really is. Or, at least, it isn't how the book that Jimmy wrote says it is. Jimmy's book follows the usual model in that he says he made the series Oscar had wanted him for and then he made two more because Susu wanted him to and he felt he owed her and, in any case, the agents were united in their advice: Don't Cross Susu. And then he branched out. He was in a lot of movies. He doesn't list them in his book because that wasn't the kind of book he set out to write, but he *did* write about three of his female co-stars and their sexual preferences. All three women are now elderly, but still alive. I thought about these passages for a long time, and then I talked to Mandrill Press's libel lawyers, and we agreed that, for the first two, I could give you the general thrust (there was a lot of thrusting) but I could not mention the films they appeared in, I should not describe the homes they lived in or say anything at all that might give the remotest hint about who they might have been. Jimmy named the women; I have not. In the version you are about to read, they are simply *A* and *B.* The third one wouldn't have cared what we published; she appears here as *C* for other reasons entirely.

I'm afraid that that means that Chapter 20 will come across as a chapter of straight porn (and Chapter 23 even more so), but the alternative is for me and Mandrill Press to be sued out of existence and we don't want that. And, in fact, much of those chapters *is* porn. Jimmy didn't love the women in them; he screwed them without affection and without feeling and, if you're looking for a definition of pornography, that would be mine.

Chapter 20
Author: James

If you make a go of it in Hollywood, you need at least three agents. One to make sure you're considered for all the parts that are going and you get your share. One to look after your financial and tax affairs. And one to take control of your life, who you meet, what parties you're invited to, what the Press says about you and, just as important, what the Press doesn't say. Marty introduced me to his agents and all three took me on. They did it as a favour to Marty, I know that, but I also know they didn't lose out financially in the end. I was never going to be a leading man but as a character actor, a best supporting actor, I was an earner.

I was also welcomed by some of the women I acted with.

A was a sort of archetype of the people I worked with. She presented to the public—what she thought of as *her* public—as a nice person. She wasn't. How could she be? Nice people don't get into the big-paying jobs (a fact I liked to remember when I was banking large cheques myself). See her on the red carpet at a premiere and she'd be smiling and waving to the fans, the star with a human face. When a star-struck girl, fifteen or sixteen, saw us walking from the limo to the latest celebrity restaurant and said, 'Can I have your autograph, please?' *A* said, 'Why don't you fuck off?' That was the real *A*.

Why was I with her? To sell the movie we had made together.

I didn't like her and I didn't pretend to like her. But in bed, I did. In bed she was like nothing I'd ever encountered.

We had just returned to her place from an evening with people like us. People with lots of money; people whose faces shone from billboards; people whose activities filled the entertainment papers. I don't believe we had the expression *paparazzi* then, but they existed. We'd been shot when we arrived at the dinner, when we left and when we got home. *A* had been gracious to them all.

That was work. That was what kept her in the big earnings league. We went through the front door and the mask came off. She gave her coat to the maid and told her she wouldn't be needed again that night and she should go to bed and not spy on us.

She went into the bedroom and from there into the bathroom. I poured myself a Scotch in the living room, threw my jacket across a chair and settled down to wait. When *A* came out, she was wearing a cotton and lace nightdress that didn't quite cover her neatly trimmed bush.

A had a strange kind of sofa I had never seen before. It looked like two chairs built together with a common back and she said it was a *boudeuse*. She also said it had been made in France about 1750 and had cost her a small fortune. *A* was prone to tell you what things had cost. The upholstery was well-padded silk damask, with gold thread tassels. Looking at it, you might think it was meant for two people to sit with their backs to each other and *A* said that, as well as *boudeuse*, the French also called it a *dos-a-dos*. *Boudeuse* meant sulky, which *A* said fitted a chair where lovers could sit with their backs to each other, and *dos-a-dos* meant back-to-back.

Sitting back to back was not what *A* used it for, however. She knelt on one half of the sofa and bent over the division between the two halves so that her ass—actually, her arse, because *A* was English—was in the air and her head hung down into the other seat. Her nightie was now up around her waist somewhere.

'Rim me,' she said.

A had the best-looking backside I've ever seen, and I've seen a few. Her waist was slim and she was pretty good above it but it was her bottom that got your attention. It was perfect. And I was looking at it.

I knelt behind her. I put my hands on her firm, unblemished behind and pressed my lips to it. A scent of peppermint and basil told me that she had been on the bidet with her organic herb soap before offering herself to me. Say what you like about *A;* she never asked you to do something you would find unpleasant. I moved slowly from the place I had kissed into the cleft and on to the

126

puckered, dark place within. When the tip of my tongue began to work itself into her she was squealing and squirming. I slapped her buttock roughly. 'Hold still, woman.'

The squirming intensified. 'Oh, Jimmy. Oh, God, Jimmy. Oh, *God, God,* **GOD!**' I nudged her knees apart and slipped my hand down, letting my thumb slide into her. She was as moist, as ready, as any woman I'd ever touched. I found her clitoris. She went absolutely rigid, her back arched like a cat's.

She rolled over. 'My pussy, Jimmy. Eat my pussy.' Then 'NO!' as my head moved down. 'The bathroom, Jimmy. Mouthwash. Please.'

That was *A* to a T. She practised safe sex before most people had heard of it. She was in desperate need but she didn't want a tongue moving straight from her back bottom to her front. That was how disease was spread.

I came back from the bathroom as quickly as I could and it was just as well because she had all five fingers buried inside her. I took them out and sucked them. Then I pushed her knees wide apart with my hands and held them there while I buried my face in her muff and my tongue in her juicy folds. It didn't take long; she convulsed and threw both legs round my head as though she wanted to crush me. When I was able to lift my face from the juncture of her thighs it was spattered in her juices. I reeked of them.

I didn't like *A* very much, but she played fair. She'd had her climax and now it was time for mine. After I had come deep inside her I got a kiss on the forehead before she stood up and made for the bathroom.

S omeone who did not play fair was *B*. She was a star and I was a supporting actor. She was Number One and I—I simply did not matter.

Ironic, then, that it was because of me that *B* received her first Oscar nomination.

It seems odd now, in this paradoxical time when anything goes and yet mainstream Hollywood has abandoned sex in movies, that *Caitlin* caused such a hullabaloo when it was made. Everyone knows that the novel it was based on wasn't called *Caitlin;* everyone knows B had the title changed to the name of her character. That's how B was. It was no big deal; Hollywood allowed stars privileges like that. Shelly Pitman, who wrote the book, didn't intend Caitlin to be the central character; B did. She pointed at me with her thumb. 'You're going to name it after *him?* Are you *serious?* Who's going to buy tickets to a movie about *him?'*

The producers agreed with her. The movie was retitled *Caitlin* and the script was rewritten to show the story the way B wanted it shown. Shelly didn't mind. She banked a lot of money from that movie.

I should think most people know about me and the terrible thing I did to B. I've never thought it worth the trouble to correct that story. It's about time to set the record straight.

In the book as written by Shelly, Caitlin was raped by my character in Chapter One and spent the next ninety thousand words slowly putting her life back together. B had a number of problems with that. First, she was against the idea of rape. Well, we all were—Shelly Pitman; B; me. Shelly and I objected to one person using violence to invade another person's body and take from them what they didn't want to give. That was why Shelly had written the book—to tell men that rape was not a male right but a dreadful misuse of a woman. B's objection was different; she didn't do sex. She'd never had a penis inside her. She didn't ever want one inside her.

The producers said they were sorry, they understood B's feelings on the subject but there had to be a rape in the first reel. They'd paid good money to secure an option on Shelly's book and they were going to film something that was at least slightly like it. If B didn't want to do a film about rape she shouldn't have accepted the offer. Couldn't she read a script? If B insisted on shooting *Caitlin* without any rape she'd be in breach of contract, they'd find another star and they'd sue *B* for wasting their time and costing them money. They didn't say, "You'll never work in this town again" because Hollywood wasn't like that any more. The studios no longer had the power they'd once had. They weren't completely toothless, either.

B listened to her agent and went through with the deal, but with some modifications to the script. She'd be raped, but the camera had to stay on her face all the time. No peeking at the action down below. In Shelly's book, the impact of the rape on Caitlin was cataclysmic; in the movie, *B's* facial expressions would show that she rose above it; that, for all the violence being done to her, she could forgive the person doing it. Then, instead of sinking into suicidal despair from which she would not emerge until the final reel, she would bounce back immediately. She would turn my character in to the police. She would do that for my sake more than for hers; I needed to confront what I was and change. I, of course, being a man and therefore deceitful, would deny my guilt and the police would not believe her; this lack of belief would continue until at the very end *B* produced the evidence that could convict me. She would present it to me and not to the police and I would collapse in sorrowful remorse.

I wasn't a big enough star for *B* to appear opposite. Really, she wanted Jean-Paul Belmondo. It was more than ten years since he had stunned cinema audiences in *Breathless* and he had just completed *Stavisky* for Alain Resnais, which led *B* to think that he would be perfect for the moody, reflective piece that she planned would make her name with foreign audiences. Foreign audiences were so much more aware than American ones. She got her agent to send the script to Belmondo. It came back quickly, which she saw as a good sign; she assured me that there would still be a place for me in the production. Something smaller. Something more suited to my talent. Belmondo had written his comments on the script; unfortunately, *B* had no French. Mine was little better, but A Level French did at least enable me to translate for her the ex-boxer's suggestion that she should stick the script up her derriere and set fire to it. I remained in the role the producers had assigned me.

As soon as we started shooting it was clear that we had a problem. B had never been the world's most accomplished actress. John Huston, attempting to direct her in *The List of Adrian Messenger,* had told her, 'Don't try to act, honey. You don't know how to do it. People buy tickets to your movies so they can see your beautiful face and those incredible tits. If they want acting, they watch someone else.'

It *was* a beautiful face and they *were* incredible tits, but that didn't help her show how she felt about being raped. As she had demanded, the camera stayed on her face and that made things worse. If she'd allowed him to film her struggles as I pulled up her skirt, the director would have got something he could use. Instead, all that went into the can was amateur dramatics. We did six takes, each hopeless. Then the director took me on one side.

'You've got to put the fear of God into her. Get some emotion onto that wooden face.'

'I'm doing my best.'

'You can't do it on the set. Get her in her trailer.'

I thought about it. 'You'll take care of me if she screams?'

'Any threats from her, I'll threaten to destroy her. We've got a fortune riding on this movie.'

'Okay.' I looked at my watch. Ten past eleven. 'Listen—call her back on set at exactly eleven twenty-five.'

'Got it.'

'Not eleven twenty-three and not eleven twenty-seven. Eleven twenty-five.'

'I said, "Got it".' He called out, 'Twenty minutes, guys.' To B he said, 'Go to your trailer with Jimmy. He has some suggestions he wants to make.'

* * *

B was rattled; she knew it wasn't going well and however hard she tried to fool herself she knew it was her shortcomings that were to blame. 'So,' she said. 'The star is expected to listen to suggestions from a nobody.'

I stepped right into her personal space. She moved back; I followed. She said, 'What do you think you're doing?'

'That's it,' I said. 'You can do the fear when you really feel it. Why can't you do it on set? Isn't that what acting is?'

'Fear! I'm not afraid of you.'

'No?' I grasped her chin in one hand and squeezed. She was up against the wall now. I pushed one knee between hers. Her hands came up to try to break my grip on her chin, but she didn't have the strength. I was still going to the gym three times a week and still careful about what I ate and drank. I was in good shape, and I was far too strong for *B*.

'Get *off* me,' she said.

I picked her up, carried her the three paces to the daybed and dropped her on it. I came down on her, grabbing both of her wrists in one hand. With the other I pulled up her skirt. I rammed both of my legs between hers and pushed my knees apart, opening her legs wide. I stole a surreptitious look at my watch. Eleven twenty-two. Three minutes still to go. I said, 'I'm going to fuck you.'

'*No!*'

'Yes.' I kissed her. It was straight out of *Actor's Manual: Cruel Kiss* section. Out loud I said, 'Someone should have done this years ago. You need a good hard shagging.'

'*No!* Please, Jimmy. *Please.* Let me up.'

I looked at the watch again. Thirty seconds to go. I ran my hand deliberately down the front of her panties and watched her shudder. There was a sharp rap on the trailer door. 'ON SET, PLEASE.'

I sat back. 'Don't think you're saved because you're not. As soon as shooting's over for the day we're back in here, just you and me, and I'm going to fuck you till you can't stand up.'

I went back on set, *B* followed me a few minutes later and the scene went like clockwork. We did the first take, the director shouted 'Cut', smiled at me and we went on to the next sequence.

When we broke for lunch, he said, 'What did you *say* to her?'

'Oh. This and that.'

'She was perfect. I'd never have believed she could act like that. The look on her face, it was like she was certain you really were going to fuck her. She was terrified.'

'Maybe I should be an acting coach.'

'Maybe you should.'

The rumours started before the movie was even finished. I had raped *B* in her trailer in order to get her to perform. The director, frustrated by *B's* inability to act, had told me to do it. It had been my own idea, fuelled by irritation at my inability to break down *B's* fabled chastity. I had simply lost control of myself when so close to such a beautiful woman. I had been drunk (or high)— industry insiders talked openly about my reliance on alcohol (or drugs). *B* had egged me on, her well-known virginity being merely a front for what other insiders knew to be insatiable nymphomania. There was no scenario and no motive that did not have its devotees.

My PR agent told me to ignore it. It would all die down and, anyway, it was good publicity and it would sell tickets when the movie was released. (It did). When I was offered the part in *Brumaire* I assumed that *B's* agent had told her the same thing.

B was already signed for the female lead in *Brumaire* opposite Vincent Scoter when we started making *Caitlin,* but Vince broke his leg the week before shooting was due to start. I'd bought a holiday house on New Providence, on the coast not far from Nassau, and I was there when a courier brought the *Brumaire* script. *B* was to play a French noblewoman trapped by Napoleon's *coup d'état.* My part was as the American who rescues her from the ruffians who have invaded her chateau and spirits her away to the coast where I have a barque waiting to carry her to a new life in Virginia. During the long voyage under sail B and I fall in love with each other and, after a passionate but chaste courtship, marry on arrival in Jamestown.

I rang my agent—the real one; the one who made sure I had enough work and the right kind of work. 'I can see a few problems with this project.'

'What? That you're not American? That B isn't French? Forget about it. The movie-going public never heard of 18 Brumaire. Most of them never heard of Napoleon, either. They think he was the man from U.N.C.L.E.'

'No, no. I'm sure we can do the accents. It's B. She isn't going to accept me for this part.'

'Jimmy, B is why you got the part. She asked for you.'

B had asked for me. I didn't know what to make of that. That day when I had, apparently, terrified her into acting by making her think I was going to force myself on her she had left the set immediately the day's shooting was over. I'd said I would follow her back to her trailer and fuck her till she couldn't stand up. I hadn't meant it, but she didn't know that and she had responded by not going back to her trailer at all. She'd given me one look, half furious and half frightened, and she'd gone. Next day she brought her maid with her and the maid spent the whole day in the trailer. Every succeeding day had been the same.

Chapter 21
Author: James

I didn't want to leave Nassau right then. The Bahamas has every racial mix you can imagine, and some of the most beautiful women I've ever seen are there. If you want proof that black is beautiful, go to New Providence and look around you. I guess you'd say Molly was genetically African, eighty per cent maybe, and the other twenty per cent might have been all sorts of things but there was a smattering of Chinese there and that Black African/Chinese combination is the most shatteringly gorgeous of all. She smiled like an angel and walked like a gazelle, but it wasn't just appearance; Molly's true glory was inside her head and inside her heart.

I thought she should be a model or an actress and I told her so. She said she was happier working in a bank. I said she could be famous and rich and she said she had everything she needed, thank you. The centre of her world was her father and mother and sister and the Baptist Church. She didn't completely rule out the idea that I might join this world, though she feared the influence of the people I moved among.

Baptist means different things to different people. A white visitor from Alabama asked where in London he could find a Baptist church and, when he came back, he was shaking. 'They were all *coons* in there,' he said. The days of a black president of the USA were still a few decades away and white people in Alabama still said coon. And nigger. And some other things, even less attractive. (Actually, they still do, but mostly not in public any more). Be that as it may, when I went to church with Molly and her family I was the only white man in the building. I asked if they didn't have a honky even as a janitor, but they didn't think that was funny.

I was serious about Molly. The plan was clear: I'd remain chaste, because Molly was not going to bed anyone until she was married to him; I'd woo her for as long as it took (sometimes I imagined the pair of us going down the aisle in wheelchairs); and I wouldn't leave the island till I'd won her.

The Elders of her church had other ideas. They came to see me in my holiday home. I made iced tea and we sat on the patio looking over the blue Caribbean while they explained the facts of life. I was wrong for Molly. If I married her it would end in disaster. They liked me personally, they were sure I was a nice man (the words "for a honky" weren't actually spoken but they hung in the air like cigar smoke) but there were already lots of nice men in their congregation who'd love to date Molly and didn't have my disadvantages. What were those? Well, I was white. I was an actor and everyone knew about the dissolute and godless lives actors lived. What about Sidney Poitier? He was different; they'd been talking about white actors. Any other disadvantages? I'd take her away from the place she'd been brought up in and knew and then she'd be exposed to temptations that were best avoided. My presence was confusing her and preventing her from seeing clearly all the other suitors lining up three abreast, their mothers standing behind them smiling their approval. They didn't want to cause me grief but nor did they want me to see Molly ever again and, just to make sure I didn't, I should sell my house, leave the island and promise never to come back.

Of course, I said No. The Pastor said that was a pity and they'd try to make sure nothing permanently bad happened to me but he worried about the more hot-headed among his flock.

They left, and I went back to reading the *Brumaire* script although I knew I was going to turn it down because it would take me away from Nassau and from Molly before my woo was done. I didn't need the money. How much can one normal person spend in a lifetime? If I never worked again I wouldn't want for anything.

That night, my house burned down. I was asleep in the bedroom at the back when the blaze started in the front, and the Elders broke the back door down and came in to wake me before the flames got me, too. They didn't explain what they'd been doing there and I didn't ask; perhaps they were holding a prayer meeting to ask God to show me the light. There was certainly a lot of it around, considering what a pitch black night it was over the rest of the island. The Pastor asked where my passport was and told me to be sure to rescue it. I thanked them for their assistance and the Pastor reminded me that he'd said they'd try to make sure nothing permanently bad happened to me and I said, 'You mean, like Death?' and he said nobody knows God's will but God and they might not be there next time something like this happened and I said, 'He really does work in mysterious ways, doesn't he? God, I mean?' and the Pastor said there was a pattern to Life that we'd see when we'd passed beyond, but the vision would be vouchsafed only to some of us. I think he meant only to black Baptists, but I wasn't looking for a theological discussion at the time.

I sleep in the nude and that's how I'd been when they hauled me out of the burning house but one of the Elders had helpfully saved a pair of slacks and a shirt while I was digging out the passport and another one grabbed a pair of sandals so I had something to stand up in. When it was light I went to Molly's house but her father said she was staying with friends. New Providence is a small island that you can drive all the way round in less than an hour so I asked where her friends lived but he said he couldn't tell me unless they agreed, and he couldn't ask them because they weren't on the phone. I asked if she'd be home that evening and he said he believed she had a date.

When I'd picked up my passport my wallet had been with it, so I had some money. I went to the Toronto Dominion Bank at ten o'clock and drew out some more. As I walked in I saw Molly and she saw me. She turned away and walked up the stairs. Only staff were allowed there. There was sadness on her beautiful face, but there was also determination.

I accepted defeat. Looking back now, I wonder if perhaps I didn't love her as much as I thought I did, but the alternative explanation is that I knew I'd been given a warning and I might not be helped to survive next time and Molly had been told to wash her hands of me and she was doing what she was told. That's the explanation I prefer. I bought a ticket to LA and, just after midnight, I was drinking a glass of wine and smoking a joint in my back yard in Venice. Next morning I rang my agent and said I'd take the *Brumaire* part.

My thoughts about Molly were that she'd realise what she'd lost and she'd write to say she wanted me back, and when she did I'd tell her to take a hike. It's very childish and it isn't very nice but it is very me. It took a few weeks for common sense to kick in and for me to realise that Molly's people didn't have much, all the wealth was in the hands of the sort-of-white and pass-for-white people known locally as the Bay Street Boys and if Molly's parents didn't much like white people they had a number of good reasons. I spoke to my lawyer and he instructed a Nassau lawyer and we conveyed the house to Molly and assigned the insurance to her. She might not value money but she was going to have some.

I didn't hear from Molly, but I got a letter from her father:

Dear Mr Carlton
Molly has asked me to thank you for your generous wedding
gift. We are having the house fixed, but Molly and her
husband won't move into it; they have bought a plot not
far from our house and they will sell the house and use the
money to build one there. Missus Brown and I are looking
forward to having grandchildren so close.
Yours truly
(Mr) Wesley Brown

I didn't believe it. It didn't fit with anything I thought I knew about Molly. I left it a year and then I got one of my agents to put a private eye on the job. He reported that the house *had* been rebuilt and it *had* been sold (for more than I'd paid for it) but that Molly had not married, that she still lived at home and that she didn't seem to be in any kind of serious relationship.

That was fine. They'd wanted me to know that she was lost to me for ever and the lie was an effective way to do that.

The investigator sent some pictures of Molly that suggested she was even more beautiful now than she had been before. I was pleased to have those photos. I haven't looked at them for many years, but I never threw them away.

I had to meet *B* again and I wasn't looking forward to it. Before that came an incident that turned my stomach.

I'd never met the woman who came to my house with her daughter. She was fortyish, fighting to hold back the years and not very well dressed and I thought maybe she'd come to ask for a job. I needed a new cleaning lady and I showed them into the kitchen and made coffee. I apologised to the daughter that I didn't keep any soft drinks in the fridge; she shook her head to say it didn't matter and asked for a glass of water.

The woman said her name was Marisca Gonzalez. She didn't look Hispanic and she didn't sound it, but Gonzalez was what she said her name was. She said, 'I've been through hard times, Jimmy.'

'Do we know each other? Have we met?'

'No. We've never met. But I feel I know you. From watching your movies, you know. You seem like a friend.'

'Well, Marisca, what can I do for you?'

'Since my husband left me, I've been sinking. If I don't raise five thousand dollars this week we're going to be out on the street.'

'I see. Does your husband know?'

'He doesn't care. He got himself another woman and we can go to hell.'

'I'm sorry. But what is it you think I can do for you?'

She looked towards her daughter, then back at me. 'I thought we might trade.'

'Trade?'

'My daughter, Trisana. She's fourteen and a virgin. That's got to be worth five thousand bucks.'

I couldn't believe what I was hearing. I looked at the girl—Trisana. Fourteen? She could be—she didn't look any older than

139

that. She was staring at the floor. Not in embarrassment; she was simply passing time till the two adults completed their negotiation. I opened the door. 'I'd like you to go.'

'All night. She'd stay with you all night.'

'I said, go.'

The girl was on her feet, ready to leave, not looking disappointed and not looking pleased; showing no emotion at all, in fact. It hit me. Was the girl—the *child*—this woman was offering not quite the full dollar? And would that make her suggestion even worse? Or not so bad? She went to the door and waited for her mother, who was not yet ready to leave. 'Are you gay?'

'If I were, would you offer me your son?'

'I've heard you might be gay.'

'Do I have to throw you out?'

'You touch me, I'll have you in court for assault.' She was making her way to the door, though; she'd given up. Or almost. 'I really do need five thousand bucks.' She looked around my kitchen. I suppose it must have looked to a poor woman like a picture in a lifestyle magazine. 'And you don't. You wouldn't notice it.'

'Have some sense, woman. I give you money after the offer you've made, you go to the Press, whose going to believe I didn't take you up on it?'

'I wouldn't let her do that,' said Trisana. This girl I'd thought might be simple was not. 'Mom needs the money. If you give it to her, I'll tell anyone who asks that you didn't touch me. I'll tell them you were really nice. You *are* really nice.'

Marisca was looking deflated. I was angry, in fact I was furious that any mother could offer her daughter to a stranger for money. She didn't know me, even if the movies made her think she did. How did she know what I'd have done to the child? Did she think a man who'd buy an underage girl for sex would treat her well? But they didn't look as though they were getting by. She'd said she was sinking and that's how she looked—how they both looked. Neither of them had had a square meal in far too long. I said, 'Sit down.' I said, 'Okay, I'm going to buy Trisana's virginity.'

The girl looked disappointed, but she swung back into the kitchen like someone who was going to do what she had to do and I said, 'Not for me. For you.'

She understood straight away and I wondered how I'd ever imagined she might be dim. To Marisca I said, 'I'm going to write you a cheque for ten thousand dollars. Twice what you asked for. What I get in return is your promise that the offer you made to me you will never make to anyone, ever again. Not even when Trisana is legal. You understand?'

She nodded. 'You're a gent. An English gentleman.'

When I'd written the cheque and Marisca had put it in her purse, Trisana came to me and held up her lips for a kiss. I said, 'Trisana. You must never kiss a man old enough to be your father unless he *is* your father.'

'But you're lovely. And I'm grateful.'

'That's fine. Show it by shaking my hand.' I held out my hand and she did shake it, though now it was clear that she was the one thinking she was dealing with someone who was differently sane.

Chapter 22
Author: James's Sister

I'm interrupting here because I want to explain what we did in the next chapter, "we" being me and Mandrill Press's lawyers.

Film buffs will have been wondering why they never heard of *Brumaire* or *Caitlin*. It's simple: we'd already encoded the name of the lead actress and we also changed the name of the film. As I said before, we didn't want to be sued. We felt that those changes were enough. *C's* case was different. Jimmy wrote about her—what kind of person she was—and he also described some of the movies she appeared in, and the result was dynamite. If we had allowed the descriptions of the films' plots to stand, no-one would have been left in any doubt about who she was. But *C* would not have cared. She is not a person who protects her privacy. That is obvious from the reference to "those nice people in Lantana, Florida" in Chapter 23; I had to look it up, but Lantana was at that time the headquarters of the *National Enquirer*, America's filth purveyor. They don't seem to have rumbled *C's* early days as a porn star, or if they have they haven't come up with the evidence to make it stick, and if this book had provided that, *C* would not have complained.

We were ready to go. And then I read IJ's report.

Talking to C *was perhaps the strangest experience of all those your brother's book has led me to. Here I was, sitting opposite a woman who had been a sort of goddess for me and my generation. I was a journalist for forty years; I believe almost nothing claimed by almost anyone; but I believed in the virtue of* C. *She, possibly alone among Hollywood's women, had remained chaste in Gomorrah. I would invite you to consider the stunning impact of your brother's revelations but I don't need to because you have read them yourself and they must have hit you as they hit me. The virgin was a whore.*

When I went to see her, I half expected that she would deny everything and expose your brother as a fantasist. She did not. She simply laughed. Yes, she said, it was true. Every word of it. I told her the book was likely to appear in the shops and she said, in effect, "Go ahead. Publish." She really didn't care what the public learned.

It was an afterthought, but I had noticed that Barbara was not present and I said I thought we really should have her approval, too. That brought about a marked change in atmosphere. C and Barbara are no longer together, and C is clearly unhappy about the break. Barbara has gone back to what C calls Nowhere, Nebraska and it was clear that I could not advise you until I had talked to her. She wasn't easy to track down. She didn't—doesn't—want to be found. Barbara is married to a man ten years older than her who has three children by a previous marriage. He owns a gas station, a dry cleaning business and a motel. He's a pillar of the town, a Rotarian and a councilman. Is Barbara happy? I don't know whether she's happy—but she's made a life and she doesn't want to lose it.

When I spoke to her, Barbara was appalled at the idea her past might be revealed. It broke her up. She talked about the disgrace it would bring on her husband's children to have it known in a town like that that their stepmother had been a porn star. She said her husband would divorce her. She'd have to move on and she says she's too old to move again. Whatever she has, she wants to keep.

Those are the facts, Katie. What you do with them is up to you. I'm glad it isn't a decision I have to make.

I thought about it for a long time. I felt quite uneasy about the way Jimmy had presented this part of his story. Am I saying that I don't approve of his frankness at other people's expense? Well, yes, I suppose there are times when I don't. Take the films out of Chapter 23 and we're left with only *C's* sex life. In effect, we end up with a soft porn chapter and soft porn is not what I want to publish. My first thought was to remove *C* from the book entirely—but in the last resort this book is an account of my brother's life: who he was in his teens; what he'd become by the end of his life; and how he got there. Jimmy started out having sex with men and women, but I don't think he's left us in any doubt that he preferred being in bed with men. In his later years the men didn't get a look in. He only wanted women. Helen had been an early sign of that change, but when she dumped him he went back to Guy and ended up with Marty Bone. He clearly enjoyed sex with Karen, he told her he preferred women and I think he meant it, but that didn't stop him dressing as Lucy and putting on a show that so excited Oscar the poor old man had a heart attack and died. He wanted to marry Molly Brown but that was not to be. When we watch him frolicking with C, though, I don't think we're watching a man who just likes sex, any sex, with any kind of partner. What we see in Chapter 23 is a man who wants women.

That's how I read it, anyway.

Barbara is still here, but so heavily disguised that only an insider—someone who knew C and knew the part Barbara (a name that's a million miles from the one her parents gave her) played in her life—will know who she is. And insiders know about her anyway. Babs, if you ever read this I hope you'll feel I've protected your privacy. I certainly tried.

Chapter 23
Author: James

Bwas cordial when I met her, which was a surprise. What had happened in her trailer was never mentioned. She told me she'd asked for me in *Brumaire* because we worked so well together. And she had something to give me. 'I saw a picture of the earth reflecting the sun's light. The earth looks beautiful, but we can only see it because the sun is there. Take away the light from the sun, no-one would ever see the earth.'

I knew the answer but I had to ask. 'And which am I, *B?*'

'Well, Jimmy, I'm the sun. Obviously.'

I know a lot of actors who would have torn up the contract at that point. I don't have that kind of ego. I was going to be paid a million bucks to make *Brumaire,* and if it pleased *B* to see herself as the sun round which my earth rotated, I could live with that.

We made *Brumaire* and *B* received her first ever Oscar nomination, for Best Actress. She didn't actually win, and in fact she never did take an Oscar home (I pretend to take no pride in the one I have (and the three nominations); I'm lying), but industry insiders were amazed that she'd even been nominated. I got the credit. I had forced her to act in *Caitlin;* I'd done it again in *Brumaire.* Susu let anyone know who would listen (and everyone listened to Susu, if only in self-preservation) that I had been her choice and I was going to be a star. She also let selected people know about my bedroom talents, which was how I came to know *C.*

Before I get on to *C,* it's only fair to say something about Hollywood people I admired. Otherwise, it's going to seem that I have nothing good to say about anyone.

It is said that, when she played baseball at school, Shirley MacLaine scored more home runs than anyone else—in a team otherwise made up entirely of boys. I have no trouble believing that. Shirley MacLaine was and is head and shoulders above every other actor in films. male or female; American or foreign; private or accessible. She is what "Star" means. Anthony Hopkins called her the most obnoxious actress he had ever worked with and Don Siegel said, "She's too unfeminine and has too much balls. She's very, very hard" but I have found her wonderful. She tells it as she sees it—never lies, never bends the truth to make people feel more comfortable, refuses to stroke male egos by acting the compliant little lady. A WYSIWYG person; there aren't many of them anywhere and they are especially few in the film business.

Lots of people will tell you how unpleasant John Wayne could be when he'd had a few drinks (and he had a few drinks every day. Often more than a few). I never saw it. I never acted with him but he saw me as a young man starting out and he was generous with help and advice. One evening in my early acting days (I was still making TV series for Susu) I was at home learning my script when a car turned up outside and the driver told me 'Mister Wayne wants to see you.' I said, 'Mister Wayne?' and he gave me a pitying look and said, 'There's only one Mister Wayne in this town.' You didn't ignore a call from John Wayne. I got into the car.

As it turned out, "this town" wasn't where we were going. It took about an hour to reach Wayne's surprisingly modest home in Newport Beach fifty miles to the south. The smell of marijuana was noticeable from the street. I'd never heard of Wayne being a pot smoker and, as it turned out, he wasn't; the joint was being smoked by his companion. Wayne had an ordinary cigarette in one hand and a glass of whisky in the other; when I came through the door he put down his own glass to pour one for me. He waved a hand in the direction of the fragrant marijuana and said, 'The man behind that cloud is Bob Altman.' Altman didn't get up or offer to shake hands but his smile was benevolent.

With no explanation at all, they put me through a series of exercises. "Walk over there." "Drink from that glass." "Light a cigarette, looking to your right at the same time." It turned out that Altman was casting Philip Marlowe in *The Big Sleep*. United Artists wanted either Robert Mitchum or Lee Marvin; Altman preferred Elliot Gould; they couldn't agree. Altman said he'd cast an unknown before he accepted the studio's choice and John Wayne had told him to take a look at me. He said, 'I've seen you on TV. You have something. And you don't walk like a goddam Limey.'

I don't know how serious Altman was about my prospects because he got his way and Elliot Gould played Marlowe. Maybe the studio backed down because they were horrified by the idea of me in the big part. But he behaved well towards me because he gave me a small part as one of the cops and paid me fifty thousand dollars for what amounted to a day's work. That was a lot more than my father earned in a year at that time, and my father had what most people would consider a good job.

John Wayne didn't have to recommend me; Robert Altman didn't have to reward me; these were acts of unconditional generosity by good men. I mentioned Robert Mitchum and Lee Marvin as the men United Artists wanted and they were two more I came to respect, as people and not just as actors. But now I'm in danger of doing what I didn't want to do, and writing a hagiographical account of Hollywood, so I'll just say that Goldie Hawn is one of the most genuine human beings you could ever hope to meet and leave it there. She built an early career on a ditziness she does not possess—Goldie is grounded, intelligent, a good friend and she sticks to her guns under pressure.

So. *C*.

Everybody knows *C*—the babe from Cowboy Country with the pale blue eyes, auburn hair and big smile. Apart from the hair colour she was the Doris Day of her time—unwavering friend to men; dependable partner of men; loyal wife of men. The adjective you'd apply most freely to *C* would be "wholesome".

Well. Hmm. Okay. Maybe.

I'd met her at several parties and she'd always had a nice smile for me, but she had a nice smile for most people. She'd never asked for my number and I wasn't in the book but she'd got it from someone—almost certainly Susu—and one evening she called me.

'What are you doing tonight?'

'Nothing.'

'Nothing?'

'Well. Not nothing. I'm going to read *Crowned Heads.*'

'I wonder if people think that's a true picture of Hollywood.'

'People?'

'Ordinary people. People who eat popcorn at the movies in Aspen, Colorado. Anyways, *Crowned Heads* will still be there tomorrow. You wanna come over?'

'You having a party?'

'I sure hope so. A party for two. A fuckfest.'

She let the silence run. When I'd got over my shock (this was the Hollywood Virgin I was talking to) I said, 'Give me your address.'

'I'll send my Girl Friday for you. I've got some real good shit and a bottle of Dom Perignon. You don't want to be driving home after that.'

The Girl Friday's name was Barbara and she was a flaxen-haired, busty woman who had once been a beauty and reminded me of a milkmaid which turned out to be an inspired insight because I found out later, when I knew her and *C* a lot better, that she had played just that part in one of the porn movies in which she and *C* had met.

'Susu bought them all up after I ate her out,' *C* told me. 'Susu has a nice cunt for an old lady. But I think you know that.'

I nodded.

'She was going to put me in Oscar's movies and she didn't want anyone digging up old dirt. Of course, you never get them all. I'm sure those nice people in Lantana, Florida are waiting for the right moment to spill the beans. But I don't care. I've made a shitload of money and I've had a good time and there'll always be someone wanting to get into these panties. Quite apart from Barbara, of course.'

That conversation was still in the future that evening when Barbara delivered me to *C's* home and took herself off to another part of the house. *C* was wearing a t-shirt that clearly had no brassiere under it and a loose pair of shorts. She had laid out a spread of salads and cheese and pretzels and slices of cold beef and smoked salmon and various kinds of fruit, and she proudly showed me the sliced up pork pie that sat on a plate in a place of honour in the centre of the table. 'The guy at the John Bull Store told me this is what English gentlemen like to eat.' She picked up a jar of Colman's Mustard and put it down again. 'He said they like to spread this on it.' She came up close to me, pressing firm breasts against my chest. 'What else do you like to eat, Jimmy?'

I knew a cue when I heard one. I took her hand. As she followed me willingly to the long chesterfield I had a sudden recall of the times I had been led by men in the same way; how I had primped like a playful young girl; how happily I had given myself. Those days were gone and they weren't coming back, but I didn't regret them. That was who I had been then; this was who I was now.

When I slid the shorts down her legs I discovered that, in addition to no bra, she had on no panties. No panties and no hair. She was completely clean shaven. She opened her legs and bent her knees as I lowered my lips to her mott, washed clean and fragrant. In the bathroom later I would see a bergamot, thyme and sage soap and that's what she smelt of. I've always been grateful to women who take the trouble to be clean for me, just as I would make the effort to be clean for them, and the taste and smell of *C* was delightful. I settled myself to lick, sliding my tongue deep into her and listening to the growing tumult above my head.

You can tell when a woman you're eating out is about to come; muscles in her stomach begin to tremble and, as she loses control, it becomes harder to keep your tongue in place and about its business. I wrapped my arms round her thighs and held on tight. *C* was screaming. Her hips reared into the air with me still tightly attached to them and then collapsed onto the chesterfield. She grabbed my head and made to pull me upwards. I let it happen. She kissed me; I assume she realised that that was her own sex she was tasting.

'Thank you. You're as good as Susu said you were.'

I decided not to say anything to that.

'What do you like, Jimmy?'

The obvious retort would have been "What does Susu say I like?" but I decided against it. 'I have pretty catholic tastes.'

'A long cock like that, fucking me from behind would be good. You wanna try it? '

'Sure.'

So that's what we did. Then we drank champagne while we ate some of the food and then we smoked a joint, after which we ate some more. Time passed in the erratic way time does when pot and munchies are involved and it was six in the morning when Barbara drove me home.

I had never expected to see Trisana again and it was with something of a surprise that I found her sitting in my garden when I came home one day. 'Can I come in?'

I had reservations, but I let her in. She unfolded a piece of paper and spread it on the table.

'What's that?'

'My birth certificate.'

I guessed what was coming. I didn't want to react but she had grown into a lovely young woman with a firm body and all the right curves and I could feel myself getting hard. 'You're eighteen, now. Right?'

'Right.'

'So how is life treating you?'

'It's good. Mom found another man and we have a nice place.'

'Good. I'm glad for you.'

'I'm dating.' She smiled at me. 'He wants to go all the way and I want to let him.'

'Well, good. Just make sure you take the necessary precautions.'

'I can't give him my virginity. It belongs to you. You bought it.'

The hardness was uncomfortable. I needed to adjust myself but I didn't want her to see me do it. 'That's okay, Trisana. I give it back to you, untouched.'

'You don't want me?'

I couldn't plead guilty to that. Even though I hadn't tugged at my erection, she must know it was there. 'Old men and young women are not a good match. Go and find your date and make him happy.'

She looked sad. 'Well, if you're sure.'

'I'm sure.' I wasn't, of course; I'd have boffed her with pleasure and it wouldn't take much to take me to that point.

'It's like a debt of honour, see? An obligation.'

'You're excused.' I wished she'd just go; the sight of her breasts swelling beneath her frilled satin blouse was getting to me. I would probably have to take myself in hand after she'd gone.

'Well. Okay, then. If that's what you want. Can I use your bathroom before I go?'

I pointed it out to her and while the door was closed I took the chance to push my hand inside my shorts and pull myself straight.

When she came out she was completely naked. I stared at her. 'Oh, Jeez. Trisana, what are you doing to me?'

'Please, Mister Carlton? Please?'

I know I should have told her to dress and go. Whatever you're thinking about my morals, I agree with you. To give in to temptation would be disgraceful.

She held out her hand and I took it. She led me out of the kitchen and up the stairs. At the first door she stopped. 'This one?'

I nodded.

She opened the door, went into the bedroom and lay on the bed, smiling at me. I undressed. I took a condom out of the drawer and laid it on the table by the bed in readiness. I knelt between her legs, put my mouth to the muskily fragrant place below her bush and brought her to orgasm with my tongue. It didn't take long. She was yelling and I wondered what the neighbours would think. Then I rolled the condom into place and took her. I felt the faint barrier of her maidenhead snap; she really had preserved her virginity for the four years since her mother had offered it to me. She had her arms tight around my back and the yelling started up again. I took my time and I knew her date would have a hard time matching the pleasure she was feeling. I hoped she wouldn't find him wanting.

When it was over I kissed her. She gave back the kiss with feeling. She lay in my arms for a while, discovering the joys of detumescence, and then she got up, went to the bathroom and dressed. She came back upstairs and kissed me on the forehead. 'Thank you, Mister Carlton.'

After she had gone I looked at the sheet and saw it stained with blood. I pulled it off the bed and took it down to the washing machine.

I didn't see Trisana again, but I saw *C* often after that first time. We were never what you'd call an item—we didn't go to parties or premieres together; we didn't feature as a couple in the Press; our names weren't linked when people talked about one or other of us. *C* won Best Actress during our time together and of course she went to the Academy Awards with a beau to receive her statuette but the beau wasn't me (and nor was he someone she ever saw otherwise, and she didn't bed him, not least because women weren't his thing)—but we spent a lot of time in each other's company, sometimes at my place but usually at *C*'s. When I sit down and work it out, I reckon we must have seen each other a hundred times in two years, which is once a week as near as makes no difference, and that in itself is interesting because if you'd asked me I'd have said it was more.

Our meetings were always about, and for, sex. There wasn't a single time we were together that we didn't have it. I think now about myself at that time and I realise how completely sex with women had taken over my life. Really by then I should have reached some kind of stability and not thought about sex all the time but I hadn't and I did. Maybe it was because of all the time I'd given to sex with men, which then I'd loved so much but now I thought had kind of been time wasted. And maybe it's just the way I was, and am. Susu told me once that the reason she knew I'd be a success in movies was because women would look at me and recognise a fuck machine (a description I tried gently to deny) and at the same time know that I would value their enjoyment as much as my own (which I think was true).

Sometimes it was just me and *C* and sometimes Barbara was invited to join in. I'd never taken part in threesomes but Barbara was even less inhibited than *C*, and *C* could be wild, and I enjoyed those times. Some of the best were when I sat on the sidelines with a cigarette or a joint and watched the pair of them going at it. Barbara was easily the stronger and she would hold *C* as she wanted her and pound *C's* backside with her hand (or a slipper. Or, sometimes—and she stood up for this—a leather belt) until *C* yelled for mercy. Barbara had a choice then: sometimes she'd have *C* (front or back, it didn't matter which) with a strap-on dildo or a vibrator; sometimes she'd grind down on *C's* face while *C* ate her out; and sometimes she'd beckon to me and I'd strip off and take possession of whichever orifice Barbara had prepared for my entrance.

Obviously there are many good memories. In one of the best, Barbara was out somewhere and *C* was playing the homemaker part she liked to do from time to time. She was at the sink, washing dishes after our meal (there was plenty of room in the dishwasher; this was an act) and I dropped to my knees behind her and lifted the knee length skirt she had on. I slipped both hands beneath the elastic of her panties. She'd dropped the sponge she was using into the water so that she could twist towards me, gently lowering herself in my direction—there was some serious moaning going on. I pulled the panties down to her knees and fingered her, one hand sliding into her warm, wet sex; the other slipping up into her bottom, just as more men than I wanted to count had once done with me. She pushed me backwards so I was lying on the floor and sat on my face. Her shrieking as I licked her to climax was something to hear. Then she had me on the floor—her on top and me on my back because she found it uncomfortable to be fucked while lying on a hard floor (and so did every woman I was ever with; I can't think why it's a staple of porn movies because it just isn't comfortable for the woman. And perhaps if you're a porn-maker that's reason enough).

I could go on. There was the time she sat on me and milked me while she talked on the phone to her agent who, she swore, did not realise I was there. The time she demanded to be tied up and treated as though I were an intruder who had come upon her in the course of a burglary (that was her idea, not mine, and I didn't tell her I'd once acted out exactly the same fantasy with Ben, but that that time I'd been the one whose panties were removed; it had been my bottom and not her sex that had been penetrated). The time...well. What does it matter? We had some great times, and they went on while I was still going to bed regularly with Susu to keep her sweet and with Karen because I wanted to and she wanted to and Karen was the nearest I'd come to being in love with since Molly...and then it stopped. The time with C, I mean; Susu and Karen both lasted a little longer. Then Susu died, which put an end to that, and Karen realised I was never going to go the final mile and marry her. She was aware of the clock ticking and though she'd dithered over the question she decided that she did want to be a mother before it was too late and so she married someone else, someone who'd pursued and wooed her without result for so long he must have been astonished when Karen told him to propose again or get out of her life, but he did propose and she accepted and so that bond also came to an end.

But the first relationship to end was the one with *C* and it was *C* who finished it. She told me it had run its course, we'd had a great time but our lives needed to be freshened up and in her experience that meant finding someone new. She said she realised that people needed a fixture in their lives but she already had Barbara which meant that I was superfluous to requirements.

As I listened I realised that she expected me to be cut up— and I wasn't. I've already said that the end of my fling with Marty wasn't the heart-breaker it might have been; the same was true with *C*. She was right. It had run its course. We'd had a great time and now we could move on.

One of the things moving on meant for me was swapping my Green Card for an American passport. I became an American citizen with pride. It wasn't just about becoming a citizen of a more prosperous, better organised nation than the one I was born into—for all its problems, America is the hope of the free world, a beacon of light in a world of darkness and I was proud to call myself an American.

I set out to get to know my new country better. I travelled all over it, from west to east and from south to north and everywhere I went reminded me of the glories of America: that there are no friendlier, more hospitable people on the face of the earth; that the tolerance of difference Britain once prided itself on is alive and well here; that there is every kind of scenery and that in America you could experience all the world has to offer without ever needing to leave.

People (and I was one of them) once thanked God for making them British and now I thanked Him for letting me become American.

God. Ah, yes. God. I'd managed this far without Him. That changed.

Chapter 24
Author: James

It was a dry, clear October day in Arizona. The temperature at midday was in the seventies (Americans don't do Celsius. Like they don't do kilometres, metric tonnes or litres) and the sun was shining in a blue sky scarcely marked by cloud. There was almost no wind. For the past three weeks the trip had taken me as far east as Oklahoma City and I'd made my leisurely way through the South Plains (where they grow more cotton than Egypt); Amarillo (it had snowed, which I hadn't been expecting); Tucumcari (home of an Indian love story that some might find fanciful); Las Cruces; and Tucson. Now I was on Interstate 10, known here as the Pearl Harbor Memorial Highway, heading for LA and my Venice Beach home.

I had just joined the Metropolitan Phoenix freeway system, which is part of I10, when I realised that all was not well. There was a pain in my chest that was spreading into my left arm. I was struggling to breathe. It felt as though one of the horses that built the West had sat on me and was refusing to roll away. It was getting worse.

At moments of crisis, old habits take over. I was in America, but instead of pulling right to get off the road I went left as I would have done in England. I ended not on a hard shoulder but on an exit ramp designated for trucks only. It was a very dangerous place to stop but I had to get out of the car. I heard the screaming of brakes and the blast from a hand held down on the horn but it didn't mean anything in the face of my struggle to stop. I was actually on my feet, doubled over against the guard rail and trying to vomit, when a Freightliner demolished my car immediately behind me.

There can be no rational explanation for what happened next. I was dead. I knew I was dead. But there was no pain at all. At first, I floated in the same blue sky that I'd been looking at in the moments before death. After a while the setting changed and I was in a park; a park in the stately home sense of trees and grass and water, shaded walks and orderly flower beds. There were people, but they weren't near me and we didn't speak.

What impressed most of all was the sense of peace. All was calm—including me. I had died and everyone fears death, or so it seems, but there was nothing to be afraid of. I'd left behind a sometimes fractious world and entered a place of happiness.

I was moving, slowly, without conscious effort, scenes opening before me. There I was, five years old, at school. I hated that school. But here I was a year later, in the new school that had opened, and I was surrounded by other children, and they were laughing and so was I.

There is no hurry after death. For those yet to experience it, that may be useful to know. Just going over the first few years of my life took weeks. I didn't take to Cubs and I left. A few years later I'd be talked into trying Scouts and I'd love it but whoever guides the dead through their initiation into the afterlife hadn't reached that point yet. They took a fairly non-linear approach, because I saw other things that came after my first Scout meetings. Playing cricket for the grammar school, which I didn't do for the first time till I was fourteen. The Headingly Test my father took me to where Freddie Truman took five for fifty-eight, bowling Richie Benaud first ball, and England won by eight wickets.

I was in bed with Ben. I had Margaret on the sofa in the Holmes's sitting room. Reggie was taking my jeans off. Margaret again. She smiled at me. 'Hello, Jimmy.' I was suffused with warmth.

I was looking at a face. Even as I write that, I know it isn't true. I wasn't looking at anything. I was *aware* of a face, or a place where a face should rightly be, but I saw nothing. A warmth, a presence, a power that enfolded and filled me at the same time. Nothing you could actually *see*.

I'd been on church parades with the Scouts. Every morning at grammar school we'd sung a hymn at the end of Assembly as the teachers filed out. I'd been through Confirmation. But those were routines; something that happened as you grew up. If you'd asked me, I'd have said I was a Christian, but if you'd asked whether I believed in God I'd have said I didn't. The idea seemed slightly ridiculous. Religion was something public figures still pretended to have when I was growing up in England, and in America they mostly claimed to have it when I was an adult, but it was for show. An expected public performance. No-one really believed that stuff. Did they?

I could never explain the weeks I'd spent as a dead man because when I woke in a Phoenix hospital with tubes seemingly in every orifice the calendar said my death had occurred only three days earlier. The doctor inspecting me said, 'You should be dead.'

'I thought I was.'

'People see medical dramas on TV and they think we can work miracles. We can't. No-one should be alive after the sort of heart attack you had.'

'A heart attack.'

'Pictures of your car have been all over the TV News. It was destroyed. So would you have been if you hadn't got out. As it is, I don't know how we've kept you alive.'

I pieced the story together over several weeks. My agent spent some time with me till she'd assessed how long I'd be unable to work. My parents had flown over when they saw the news on Tyne-Tees Television; when I was discharged they came to Venice with me. My father had to go back to work after a few days but my mother was determined to stay till I was fully recovered. 'Or dead,' I said.

'Recovered,' she said, very firmly. She went food shopping every day and came back with stories of American supermarkets.

'They have a salad counter as long as our street at home, with stuff I've never seen before. Every so often, Handel's Water Music starts to play and a spray of water keeps all the lettuces fresh!'

I said, 'There's nowhere like that in Venice.'

'One of your neighbours gave me a lift. She said there was great shopping in Los Angeles and she had to get some things.'

'Where? *Where* in LA? And *what* neighbour? You can't get into cars with people you don't know! This is America. *Anything* can happen. Don't you watch the movies?'

She didn't know what neighbour. She didn't know where in Los Angeles. But a couple of days later, a local paper provided the answers.

Exclusive Interview with Jimmy Carlton's Mother
On Tuesday morning your reporter was privileged to spend some time with Mary Carlton, here to look after her son as he recovers from a massive heart attack. Getting to know Mary makes it easy to understand how much-loved character actor and Oscar winner Jimmy Carlton became the engaging man he is.
"Jimmy was a lovely boy. He always made friends easily. His father and I have been amazed, though, at the things he's done with his life."
She never thought he'd be an actor. "If we expected anything, he'd be an academic." She laughs in that self-deprecating way the British have. "I never understood where he got his brains from. Or his looks."
Mary has seen every movie Jimmy has been in and loved them all. She has only one regret. "I'm lucky to have two grandchildren by my daughter, because Jimmy's forty now and I don't think he's going to give me any. There have always been women in his life. He fell for a girl called Margaret before he'd even left school. When he was at the BBC he was with a lovely young woman and I really thought we'd hear wedding bells. Helen, her name was. And now he's here and we see photos in the papers at home. Jimmy with this starlet; Jimmy with that actress. But nothing comes of it. I just hope

when he gets to the end of his life he doesn't regret what he's missed out on."

Their son's career has amazed his parents. They put it down to serendipity, though the expression Mary used was 'winging it.' "There was no plan. It just happened. Jimmy went from one thing to another and then another and just accepted what turned up."

My mother was furious. 'I thought I was talking to a friend! I'd never have said those things about missing out on grandchildren if I'd thought they'd be made public.'

I shrugged. 'That's what journalists do. You get used to it.'

'Well, I think it's dishonest. And disgraceful. She's not a nice person.'

When I'd left hospital, they'd given me a diet sheet. I don't know why; what was on it was not so different from what I ate anyway. I said, 'Did you find my cholesterol raised?'

The doctor shook his head.

'Too much fat in my system? Arteries clogged? High blood pressure?'

'Nothing.'

'So what caused my heart attack?'

'We don't know.' He was looking at me oddly. Not bemused exactly, but something was troubling him.

I said, 'I don't eat a lot of fried food. No French fries. In fact, I hardly eat potatoes at all. I go to the gym three times a week. I don't drink much alcohol.'

'Maybe that's it. Your body was tired of such a boring life. I'm sorry, I shouldn't be flippant. Mister Carlton, we don't know what caused your heart attack. And it troubles us. It should not have happened. You smoke?'

'The occasional cigarette. A cigar once in a while.'

'Anything else?'

'You want me to incriminate myself?'

'That's answer enough. Do you take any drugs beyond marijuana?'

'Never. I never have. I probably never will.'

'And you'll probably never have another heart attack.'

"Probably" wasn't enough. My agent sat me down and explained the facts of life. 'Everybody who appears in a film is insured.'

'I know that.'

'Even the clapper. The producers take out insurance on everyone.'

'I said I know that.'

'Obviously, the most important people have the most insurance. And the biggest premiums.'

'Obviously.'

'The Director. The stars. You.'

I knew what was coming, but I was going to make her spell it out.

'You're no longer insurable, Jimmy.'

Here it was. Just like the end of my BBC career fourteen years earlier, my life in movies was being terminated—and not by me. 'Did Keystone insure Chaplin?'

'Don't make it difficult, Jimmy. You're a friend, not just a client. I don't like this any more than you do.'

'What about Buster Keaton?'

The concern on her face was replaced by irritation. 'Those were different times. Now it's all about risk assessment, and with you the risk is too great. If no-one will insure you, no-one will employ you.'

'The doctor said I'd probably never have another heart attack.'

'The doctor said no-one knew why you'd had the one you did have. That's what's done the damage.'

I could have gone on fighting it, but for what purpose? She

was right; it was over. There was no reason I shouldn't live another forty years but no insurance company could be sure I wouldn't die tomorrow. I said, 'Okay,' and watched relief come over her.

'You can still call me any time, Jimmy.'

'Okay.'

'But the person you really need now is your Business Agent.'

A lot of people have been screwed by business agents. Some lost everything they'd earned. Ten years after my heart attack, Leonard Cohen—who had thought he had five million dollars in the bank and his agent was his friend—discovered he had almost nothing. He was far from alone. I went through my accounts and found that I was in good shape. The company the agent had registered for me was in my name and only mine. It owned the title to the five buildings I had bought, each of them was rented to good tenants with rental income exceeding mortgage payments and they had all risen in value since I bought them. The shares, bonds and cash I thought I should have, I did have. My taxes were paid. I was worth about eleven million dollars in all.

I said thank you to the agent, wrote him a cheque for twenty-five thousand dollars as a thank you, and told him I'd look after things from then on. He seemed hurt. I said, 'Bennie, I have to have something to do. I can't make movies any more. I'll manage my investments.'

'Well, if you put it like that. Any time you want advice, call me.'

I promised I would.

So there I was, early forties, a millionaire a few times over, starting on a new life with not a care in the world if you discount the knowledge that never quite left me that a man whose had one heart attack that no-one can explain can have another.

I took as much care as I felt was reasonable. Even though

it took me a week to get through a pack, I dumped my cigarettes in the pedal bin and have never bought another. I gave my cigars away—I had to be careful who I gave them to because they were Cohibas, the genuine Cuban brand and not the United Tobacco version, and illegal in the US. I stuck to the kind of food I'd been eating, which wasn't far from the hospital's diet sheet.

Walter had retired a couple of years earlier and the gym was now in the hands of his son, Walter Junior, who was taking it up market. He'd already got rid of the boxing ring and the ex-cons had gone with it. He'd brought in rowing machines and steps and the rest of the Nautilus gear. He made it clear that he had nothing against gays, so long as they didn't importune or otherwise offend his straight clientele (in which he included both me—correctly, now—and Marty, which raised the odd smile among those in the know). Most rewarding of all, he had cleared out the adjacent building, which no-one had realised Walter owned, knocked doors through into the gym and installed a swimming pool, sauna and changing rooms.

He had also hired two personal trainers, one of whom put me through my paces before recommending a fitness programme.

I swam off Venice Beach. I bought a bike and cycled regularly to Santa Monica and, sometimes, as far as Malibu.

When I wasn't attending to my health I managed my investments. I sold three buildings, putting the money into beachfront property near enough to home that I could walk there.

And, through all of this, there was the background that never quite went away.

Chapter 25
Author: Jimmy

I said that when I'd been dead, or thought I was, I'd been aware of a presence, a power that enfolded and filled me at the same time. Nothing you could actually see, but it was there. I read up on the subject, Googled it and went to the library, and what I found was reassuring. Having an after-death experience didn't mean there was a life after death. Or a God, for that matter. Science could explain everything. Brains are pushed into a higher state of arousal at the brink of death, and that can trigger visions. When you're dying, the pineal gland releases a huge amount of a psychedelic drug called DMT, which induces hallucinations. As the flow of blood to the heart shrinks, the occipital and temporal cortices are affected. I had to Google occipital and temporal cortices, too, and I still don't think I really understand what they do but that didn't matter; other people did, people who were cleverer than me and they had shown there were physical, earth-bound reasons for the feelings I'd had and that was good because it meant I could forget about them. I didn't have to change the way I lived my life to accommodate some outmoded answer to the question Why Are We Here? It was a pointless question—the only sensible answer was Because We Are.

Walter jnr pointed out that I wasn't moving with my usual fluency after my heart attack and he sent me to an osteopath. 'She's a Buddhist, but she knows what she's doing.'

'She can be anything she likes. I'm not going there for religious discussions.'

His expression was odd. Odd as in devious. Tricksy odd. 'Of course you're not.'

For several weeks, various parts of my skeleton were pushed around and things improved. I asked the osteopath what she thought had happened.

'You had a physical shock as well as a medical crisis. Maybe the car caught you when the truck hit it, even though you think it didn't. Maybe it was the tension—there's bound to be a freezing up if your body thinks it's dying. How do you feel now?'

'I feel good.' And I did. Better than I had for years, in fact.

'Physically good? Or all over good?'

'There's a difference?'

Her hands lay gently on each side of my head. 'Don't hide from the truth, Jimmy.'

I didn't say anything. I wanted to, but I was afraid.

'It's written all over you. You saw God. Didn't you?'

My mouth was dry. 'You can't see God. There's no such person. God doesn't exist.'

She went on with what she was doing. 'Of course not. How silly of me.'

If you're in LA and you want a church, there's no shortage of places to pick from. In a six month period, I must have checked out fifteen. In the end, I suppose it was natural that I should settle on an Episcopalian congregation. You end up in the church where you feel comfortable. My religious background, so far as I had one, was Church of England and the Episcopalians are as close to that as makes no difference. They even use the Book of Common Prayer. In the early days I sat in the back, didn't talk to people and left as soon as the service was over. They weren't having that. I was drawn in. I joined the Men's Society. I cooked burgers at parish barbecues (parishioners, especially the women, loved having a cook who they'd seen on TV and at the movies—though I was far from being the only Hollywood name there). I talked to the priest. One day I settled down in his study and told him my story.

He said, 'There are many rooms in my father's house.' Sometimes I wished religious people would speak a little less cryptically. I asked him what he thought I should do.

'We don't give absolution here in return for telling the rosary and ten Hail Marys. If you want that, you need to try the Catholics down the road. I can give you a note to Father Murphy if you like?'

Levity I didn't need. 'What I *want* is to find my way to God.'

'Lots of people want that. They've been writing books on the subject at least since the time of Saint Augustine. It can't be done.'

'What?'

'You don't find God, Jimmy. He finds you. He's been holding out His hand to you all the way through this sorry life you've described to me. Just like he does to everyone. All you have to do is take it.'

'You make it sound so easy.'

'It is easy. The secret is in submission.'

I almost choked. Right back on the third page of this book I said, "What I dreamed of most of all was submission." I guessed the submission the priest was talking about was not the same as I'd meant back then. I said, 'How do I do that?'

'You put Him first. You pray.'

'I've never found prayer easy.'

'That's because you haven't known how. Most people only pray when they want something. That's no good.' He pushed a yellow lined pad and a pen across the table. 'Write this down. Your first prayer every morning should be: "Oh, Lord, have mercy on me, a sinner. Lord God, I place myself in your hands, for you know better than me what I really need." Then you can ask for something you want, as long as you think He'd approve. Then you say Amen. And then you say, "Father I'm sorry for my sins. Forgive me, and help me to sin no more. Bless those I have hurt in my sinning, especially..." and then any names you think would be appropriate in that context.'

'Hold on, you're going too fast for me. Okay. Next?'

'Then Amen again. The third prayer goes, "Lord, I thank you from the bottom of my heart for all the blessings you have heaped upon me, which I know I have not deserved, and for the prayers you have answered. May your holy name be glorified forever. Amen."'

He waited while I got all the words down. 'The fourth prayer is the Lord's Prayer. I take it you know the words to that?'

I nodded.

'That's it, Jimmy. But you put Him first. You say the prayers out loud and on your knees and before you do anything else.' He grinned. 'Actually, you should take a piss before you pray, just so your mind is on the words you're speaking. But nothing else. Don't get dressed, don't take whatever medication you're on, don't eat breakfast till your prayers are said. At night before you sleep you pray again. Just two prayers this time: the one thanking God for his blessings and the Lord's Prayer. And in the meantime as you go through the day and live your life you think about God and what He would want. You put Him first.'

'What does He want?'

'Don't you listen to a word in church? "You shall love the Lord your God with all your heart and with all your soul. And you shall love your neighbour as yourself." Show you're putting Him first by putting other people first. His hand is always stretched out towards you, Jimmy. Reach out and take it.'

'If I do all that I'll go to Heaven?'

'Oh, Jimmy. No-one knows what comes after death. Live as though you were living for God. That's all you can do, and all He asks. You will certainly receive your reward in this life. If there's another later, that's a bonus.'

There's something about church that makes people feel sexy. Perhaps it was that Baptist aura that made Molly so desirable. Whatever, I didn't lack propositions. Women invited me home for a meal, out for a drink or to squire them to parties. More than once, the invitation to share a bed was scarcely disguised at all. I was no longer the callow young man who'd accepted any suggestion from either sex and I steered every conversation away from the initial subject. None of them came from someone I wanted a long term relationship with and I was through with one night stands. I was still evaluating what putting God first actually meant—how in practice you did it—but I thought casual sex was probably not what He wanted (assuming He actually existed—I was still not completely convinced).

Invitations continued to come, too, to Hollywood parties and that surprised me; I'd expected that I'd be dropped as soon as people knew my acting days were over and I could no longer be any use to them.

Then I began to write.

It wasn't as clear cut as that. I didn't sit down and think, "I'll be a writer". What happened was that I heard someone say, 'How do I know what I think till I hear what I say?' and although I know now that it was not an original thought, at the time it was a revelation. Here was my route to the light. I'd dictate a story based on my own experiences and reading it when it was typed would help me understand the life I had been leading. Very quickly I realised that there was no-one to whom I'd be prepared to dictate some of the stories I wanted to record so I changed the plan: instead of dictating a story I'd write it. I did not realise when I began that I would end with a collection of more than thirty stories and that I would go on from there to write this book.

I hadn't a clue how to go about it so I enrolled in a creative writing class. I had been an A level English student, I had a History degree from a university that marked down badly written essays and I'd worked for the BBC so I knew the difference between "your" and "you're", "there" and "their" and the other word pairs that confound so many. I knew how "refute" differed from "reject" and "partake in" from "participate in". I understood where apostrophes went and where they didn't. What I didn't know was how to structure a story, how to create believable characters with their own voice, why adverbs could kill a sentence or when I was using too many words to say what I had to say. The class helped me with that.

There were eight of us and the first exercise was to write a scene in a story defined by the teacher. I hadn't even realised that chapters were broken down into scenes, but I could relate it to my work in the movies. She told us about Point of View and explained that a single scene must be written through the eyes of only one of the participants. I thought I understood that. When it was my turn to read my scene, all of the other students thought it was fine. The teacher did not. 'From whose viewpoint are we seeing this scene, Jimmy?'

'Mary's.'

'Mary's. Just so. And you maintain that through almost the whole of the scene. But in the very last sentence you say, "Tom felt as though he had been kicked in the teeth." How could Mary possibly know what Tom was feeling?'

'She couldn't.'

'She couldn't. So what's it doing in a scene of Mary's?'

This was going to be harder than I had thought.

I could fill many chapters with what I learned in that class, but the reader I imagine for this book is not looking for a writing primer so I'll just say that before I had my collection of thirty stories I destroyed forty more because what I had learned made me aware of their faults. The first one I kept was called *The Perfect Solution* and when I had finished it I knew that what I was actually doing was making preliminary sketches for this book that I hadn't even known I was going to write.

Chapter 26
Author: James's Sister

*T*he *Perfect Solution* was the first thing of Jimmy's I published. I found it in Folder 3 on his laptop and when I read it I was in tears. *The Perfect Solution* is a romance (which in itself surprised me) and it has a lovely boy-gets-girl ending that might have been designed as a tear-jerker and possibly was. Jimmy had learned to use his material to take hold of the reader's emotions. The second reason I cried was personal to Jimmy. This is how *The Perfect Solution* ends:

There is nothing in this book about "mighty love-hammers" or "thrusting thighs" because I wanted to write a story about love. Love, even sexual love, is not about those things. It's about tenderness. Affection. Closeness. Intimacy. When two people who love each other come together to make love, they become one person. Self is put aside. Sex without love is a waste of time. Trust me: I have had enough of it to know.

Why did that make me cry? Because Jimmy never reached his ideal. As he says, he'd had a lot of sex without love; he enjoyed it at the time but by the end of his life he knew it for what it was—a waste, not just as he says of time but also of what he could have been, what each of us could be. Love was offered to him—by Margaret Holmes, by Helen, by Karen. It was offered unconditionally and you sense that he wanted to accept it but he always held back. He never did put self aside or commit to another so that they became one person. That seems to me to be worth my tears.

Maybe it's the difference between men and women. Or perhaps it was just Jimmy.

When the crying was over, I reread *The Perfect Solution* and then I read it again. He refers in it to "the only woman I ever truly loved." He has told us that his stories were a way to understand his life. So who was she? Molly? A dream? An ideal woman invented to write a story around? Or flesh and blood, a woman he knew in real life and from whom he turned away, or who turned away from him? If so, she never appears in this book and I'm left wondering what else he didn't tell us.

Jimmy was a broadcaster, a writer and a lay brother in a monastery, but most of all he was an actor. He was also gay at a time when that was not possible in public. My husband and I were out for dinner a while ago and four men came in—two old and expensively dressed but the other two young and exuberantly gay. As they were shown to their table, one of the young ones said, 'How do you want us? Boy-girl-boy-girl?' Jimmy could never have got away with that during the days of his gayness. The law would have swallowed him. Marty Bone told him, 'You're acting all the time. Your whole life is an act.' He himself says he pretended to be someone else as a defensive shield. Now I find myself looking at the curtain that divides us from the place where he has gone and thinking, "You have seemed to be so open with us. What other secrets did you take with you to the grave?"

Chapter 27

Author: James

I followed the priest's instructions and prayed every day, morning and night. After a while, I added a prayer of my own: "Lord, grant me peace. Amen." I don't doubt that many people would have exchanged all the peace in the world for the material advantages I had, but Molly had been right: material things don't bring happiness. I know that's easy to say when you have plenty, but I had the material things and I know it's true.

I wanted peace because, the more I asked God to forgive my sins, the more conscious I became of what I had done.

(If you're embarrassed or irritated by the way I bring God into this—and I know a lot of people will be—substitute a word or idea of your own. I felt I was talking to God and that God was listening to me. If you feel happier just trying to be at peace with yourself, your neighbour and the world around you, that's fine by me. There's a Judge and you'll face Him one day but He isn't me).

When I talk about the weight of my sins, I don't mean the things I did; I mean the spirit in which I did them. Going to bed with Ben and Marty didn't seem worse to me than making love to Margaret or Helen or Karen, however many people might think it should, because I had done that in a spirit of affectionate giving. I wouldn't dress as a girl again or dance around men flicking up my skirt to show my knickers and I wish I hadn't done it then, but that's because I find the memory ridiculous and not because I think it imperilled my immortal soul. That's assuming that a soul is immortal. But boffing an actress I didn't like in order to sell tickets to a movie? Bad. Leaving Margaret in the lurch when I'd fathered a child on her? Bad. Taking what Karen offered while being careful to ignore her hopes that we would be together always? Bad.

The idea of praying for peace came to me in the parish men's discussion group. It met every week and I found that I was becoming franker about my troubled soul at each meeting. There was another man there who had none of what I had; he was married with three children and a low paid, menial job and

I knew that every day was a struggle financially and yet both he and his wife—and their children—were always calm. They simply accepted whatever blows life inflicted and got on with it. I looked at them with envy. When I asked where he found the peace that ruled his life he said, 'I ask God for it. What else?'

Prayer was something we talked about a lot in the group. Men more secure in their faith than me agreed that all prayers were answered (though sometimes the answer was "No" and that meant what you had asked for was wrong) but the answer never came in the form you expected.

Example: Wayne's daughter was diagnosed with a rare disease that was curable but only at an expense he could not afford. He had no insurance. He prayed for the money to pay the hospital's bills, without which they wouldn't let his daughter through the door. The money never came. But then on the bus home from work he picked up a discarded Readers' Digest and read that the diagnosis was often mistaken and the condition that doctors thought was fatal sometimes responded to a simple regimen of readily available drugs. He took the magazine home, tried the drugs and his daughter recovered.

Example: Harry lost his job. He had a mortgage that was too high and was financing his son through college. Either the house had to go or the son must leave school. Like Wayne, he prayed for money and he spent his last fifty dollars on lottery tickets. Also like Wayne, the money never came and every one of his tickets was a dud. He went on praying, this time not for money but simply saying, "Help me, Lord." His phone rang and an old boss who had retired and gone to live in Hawaii said, 'I'm back. I couldn't stand it. I'm starting up again. Any way you can be available?'

We heard stories like that every week and my reaction was the same as any normal person's would probably be: the positive results were blind coincidence. They'd have happened anyway. God had nothing to do with it. But then my sister called to say Dad had been in an accident at work and was not going to survive and if I wanted to see him before he went I'd better get on a plane right now—tomorrow would be too late. I rang every airline that flew to England but it was the first day of Wimbledon and every single flight for two days was full. Attempts to route myself through Amsterdam, Paris or Frankfurt met with the same result. I put myself on standby without hope and I prayed—not, "Please let my father survive"; not "Please find me a seat"; but "Lord, I place my father in your hands. Please take care of him." I spoke to Katie two or three times each day and the news was gloomy. 'He's hanging on but he's in a coma.' 'They don't think he'll wake again.' 'He lost too much blood.' I kept repeating the prayer, probably thirty times a day.

Forty-eight hours after I'd got the news I flew to Heathrow, rented a car and drove to the hospital. It took three hours, breaking the speed limit constantly, and I texted Katie as I pulled into the car park. I had no British coins and I needed her to put money in the meter. She came flying out of the hospital door, her face one big smile. 'He woke up this morning! He's talking to everyone!'

As we approached the ward there were shrieks from the nurses. 'It's true! It's him!' Katie said, 'He's been telling all the nurses his son is *the* Jimmy Carlton.'

The old man welcomed me with an enormous grin out of a pale, exhausted face. I said, 'They told me you were dying.'

'Tsk. People do exaggerate.'

When Katie and I left, the nurses were lined up with sheets of paper and duty rosters, asking for my autograph. One even had the wrapper from an incontinence pad. I signed with pleasure.

We brought Dad home at the weekend and he and I sat side by side all week, watching tennis on television. The British challengers had all been knocked out by the third round, but that didn't matter.

Dad went back to work. He did die—eventually. It was eighteen years after his accident and what took him away was simple old age. He had said to me while we watched the tennis, 'Life is an arc. You don't realise it when you're young, but that's what it is, and I'm on the downward slope. When you get to my age you know it might be tomorrow and it might not be for thirty years, but that's the finishing line you're looking at. Make peace with yourself before that time comes.'

When I took the car back to Avis they presented me with a speeding ticket issued on the day I drove to the hospital. I paid with a smile.

There were sage nods when I told my story at the men's group. 'When you need God's help, don't tell him what to do. Just place your problem in his hands and ask him to look after it. It doesn't matter how many billions there are in the world; he's listening. He'll hear you.'

I'd been attending that church for eighteen months when the priest invited me to his study again. 'Every week we make the sign of peace. You join in. Do you ever feel any?'

'Peace? No.'

'Jimmy, you need to remove yourself from the world for a while. You need to spend some time with God.'

'How do I do that?'

He pushed a piece of paper across the table. It had a California address on it, in a remote county. I said, 'What's this place?'

'It's a monastery. I've been talking to the Master. He's expecting you this weekend.'

'How much have you told him?'

'Everything I know.'

The monastery had been built seventy years earlier in open fields and a small town had grown up around it. The man they called the Master was sixty when I arrived on Friday afternoon and had been there for thirty years, first as a lay brother, then as a novice and then as a monk. He had been Master for ten years. When I asked who had put up the money to buy the land and build the Monastery he answered 'God' in a tone that suggested it was a pointless question. He explained what would happen during the weekend I was there.

'We work seven days a week, so our weekends and weekdays are almost the same. The work is to keep us alive, fed and housed and free from temptation; the purpose of being here is to allow God to take the place he craves in our hearts. Nothing else matters.

'We wake at five each morning when the lights come on. We have our own generators and they have never failed in my time here. If they do, a bell will be rung. For seven hours we live and work in silence because the rule is total silence until dinner. You will find a bathroom attached to your room and when you wake you should rise immediately, shower and dress. Please observe the rule of silence. You should then kneel and pray. I understand you have your prayers already. When you feel that your prayers are complete, you should read. You will find a bible and a number of religious books in your room. Please don't read anything you may have brought with you.'

I nodded.

'At six you will hear a hand bell. Walk to the refectory. Others will be making the same journey and you should not communicate with them, not even to nod hello. You will find that breakfast is filling; this is not the Middle Ages. There will always be oatmeal, boiled eggs and a choice of excellent bread from our own bakery. At this time of year tomatoes are in season and they will be served. Most of our residents have never tasted such good tomatoes— or such good eggs—until they come here. On Wednesdays and Sundays there will also be slices of fried ham. Help yourself from the sideboard as you see others do. There will be jugs of water, jugs of milk and glasses on the table and the monk in charge of tables will serve coffee. Only one cup is permitted because caffeine can interfere with contemplation and there will be no more during the day. Eat your breakfast in silence.

'Then we go to work. As a visitor you will not be required to work, but if you wish to join us we can use you in the garden.'

'I would like to work.'

'Good. Brother James is The Gardener and he will take you with him and show you by sign language what you are required to do. At nine and again at ten thirty you will be brought a drink of water. Our drinking water comes from our own well and you will find it good. At twelve you will hear a bell ringing and you will be free to speak, but please do not insist on speaking to anyone who makes it clear that they wish to continue in silence. Go to your room and wash and then return to the refectory where we will be led in prayer. Then dinner. That is the main meal of the day and you will find the food simple but plentiful. One of the brothers will read aloud from the bible. We consider it the worst of bad manners to speak at that time. Dinner lasts forty-five minutes and then back to work. Water will be served during the afternoon. Conversation is allowed. The bell will ring again at four and you should return to your room, pray and read for one hour. That is a time for contemplation and to open our hearts to what God wishes to say to us. At five the bell will summon you to the refectory where we will pray again and then eat a meal of bread, cheese, fruit and milk or water. On Sundays there will also be cake. We make a very good rich fruit cake here.

'From six until ten is your own time. Some of the brothers play chess, or simply talk; others go to their rooms to write letters home; some walk in the gardens; some go to the chapel to pray and contemplate. I understand that you like to write and you are free to do so then. No-one will read what you have written. Whatever else you do, that is the time to clean and tidy your room. If any cleaning materials are missing or exhausted, write down what you need and leave the note in the box just inside the refectory door. Don't forget to write your name; no-one here is psychic. Every Monday and Thursday clean bedding is left outside each door and the brothers exchange it for their used bedding which will be collected by a lay brother and taken to the laundry. At five to ten the bell will ring and you should go directly to your room because five minutes later the light will go out. If there is no moon, it can be very dark here. Pray in darkness and then sleep.

'On Sundays the morning routine is the same as on other days but after dinner we have a service in the chapel and then stay there for three hours of silent contemplation. No alcohol is permitted at any time, and no nicotine. Of course, no drugs. Only one newspaper comes into the Monastery and I inform the brothers of any news I think they should be aware of. That is not to keep people in the dark but merely to leave their minds unencumbered so that they can know God more readily. There is no television or radio here. We have a room where brothers can receive family visits on Sunday afternoons and there is often excited chatter after that. Usually about the latest baseball, football or hockey results but sometimes in moments of national crisis graver news is discussed. But we discourage political debate. There is a room with a telephone from which brothers can make one call a week for a maximum of ten minutes. The limit is to control the cost. That telephone will not make calls to numbers outside the mainland United States.

'Anyone found with a woman in his room, or sexually importuning another resident, will be ejected immediately without discussion or the chance to defend himself.'

'Does that ever happen?'

'Not once in my time here. Of course we know of the things that monks in Europe got up to in centuries past, but they were often not there by choice and had no vocation. We are, and do. And all of our residents are here because they wished to leave the world and its temptations behind them. We do not accept anyone who has not already lived at least ten years in the world as an adult. Anyone wishing to join us permanently must serve as a lay brother, during which he can leave at any time. After five years he may choose to undertake a five year novitiate, which he can also bring to an end, before being accepted into brotherhood. We make no charge for the kind of visits you are engaged in but donations are accepted. Anyone joining us permanently is not required to hand over his personal wealth but he must leave it behind and undertake not to call on it during his time here. And please note that word "permanently". This is not a place for sabbaticals. Any questions?'

I shook my head.

'Then one of our lay brothers will show you to your room. I hope you will find here the peace you seek.'

I had five hundred dollars in my wallet and when I left on Monday I gave four hundred and fifty to the Master. The rest was for gasoline and lunch.

Driving home, I was aware of a feeling that I could not remember ever having before. I can't explain it and I don't really want to try. It was as though (and I see I *am* trying) I had been surrounded all my life without knowing it by a separate world of calm and peace, a world that was in the world but not of it, and all I had needed to tap into it was time for quiet contemplation in a place where others were doing the same thing. The hard physical work had helped; the lack of alcohol and caffeine had helped; the lack of female temptation had helped; but what worked most of all was the hours I had spent in prayer, reading and opening my heart to God. The priest had told me that God's hand was always outstretched and all I had to do was reach out and take it. Now I felt that hand in mine.

Insanity? Self-delusion? Perhaps. I liked it, though. Liked it enough to want to hold on to it.

I told the group at our next meeting about my weekend at the monastery and how I had felt at the end of it. I still felt that way four days later. I said I thought it was the knowledge that all the people around me, everyone in the place, was thinking about God.

The priest said, 'Jesus said, "When two or more are gathered together in my name, there will I be also." And it's true. That's what is so valuable about the Church. But a church is not a self-help group, and neither is a monastery. It's good to have support but in the end our relationship with God is personal. What a church can do is help you stay on the straight and narrow. Lots of people say,

"I'm a Christian but I don't need to be in church". They make it hard for themselves and so many drift into strange ideas that make them feel good but have nothing to do with eternal life. You need both—the church or the monastery to pass on the wisdom of two thousand years, and quiet contemplation of the mystery of life to help you find your own personal road.'

I felt embarrassed to be the centre of attention, which was a strange way for an actor to feel, so all I said was, 'Well, anyway, the peace was wonderful.' Americans still looked at me oddly when I said anyway instead of anyways.

Chapter 28
Author: James

My life changed. I still lived in Venice, still walked on the boardwalk and cycled to Malibu, still wrote my stories and went to the gym but it was a different me who did those things. I went on praying and I spent two or three hours each day in quiet contemplation. I stopped drinking coffee and didn't touch alcohol or smoke weed. I didn't go on dates or accept invitations to parties. I had a sense of getting ready, but first I needed to give myself some extra time.

I collected brochures from travel agents, not to book a package holiday but to get an idea of where I might like to go. Then I went on line. Air New Zealand flies from LA to Auckland and I booked a one way ticket. When I checked visas I found that I didn't need one, but I did need evidence of an onward booking so I also booked a flight on Emirates from Auckland to Dubai.

I knew the old joke about the British Airways pilot who says, 'Ladies and Gentlemen, welcome to Auckland. Please set your watches back fifty years.' It was accurate, but not in the way you might expect: Kiwis are polite in the way the British once were and are no longer. They were open and friendly—a chip off the old British block, but now more like Americans than like people from the old country. I also liked the way they began every answer with "Look." 'Why do you see so many elderly machines here?' 'Look, every New Zealander is at the most one generation away from being a farmer, and farmers make do and mend. That's what they do. Look, it's part of the culture.' 'This is a small country. How does it produce the best rugby team in the world?' 'Look, because it's so small, every boy grows up thinking he could one day be an All Black.'

Then there was their attitude to their larger neighbour across the Tasman Sea. When I came out of the terminal on the way to collect my rental car I saw a blue line painted on the ground and I asked the woman from Hertz what it was for. 'It's to show the way from the international to the domestic terminal. Look, we put it there so Australians won't get lost.'

I'd flown Business Class, which on Air New Zealand meant upstairs on a 747, but I had decided to stay in motels wherever possible. I'd eat out and use launderettes to wash my clothes. All the motels had ironing boards in the room.

I slept well the first night and next morning I discovered two of New Zealand's finest things—the bakery breakfast and the coffee. Only Italy makes better coffee than NZ. That proved true wherever I was. I hadn't been drinking coffee but now I went back to the monastery habit of one a day. Before long, one became two. It took willpower to hold it at that. As for the breakfasts, all towns of any size had bakeries that sold muffins and croissants and other stuff freshly baked that morning, but what stood out about them was that many also sold full English breakfasts. Apart from when I was home after Dad's accident, I hadn't had one of those since I'd moved to America. Americans don't understand bacon, just like they don't understand coffee. You could eat inside or at tables on the pavement (I had to get used once more to the idea that, as in Britain, what Americans call a sidewalk is a pavement).

It took me a week to drive to Napier, where I was planning to leave the car. On the way I saw Lake Tahoe and I lunched every day at a vineyard. That's when I realised that the breakfasts weren't an accident; Kiwis love food and they're very good at it. I thought I had given up wine but what they make in NZ is good, I was on what might well be my last ever holiday and I allowed myself two glasses of whatever the local wine was with lunch. That meant I had to rest afterwards and then find a motel to stay in, which accounted for my slow progress.

I wanted to see Napier because it is an *art deco* down, completely rebuilt in the 1930s after a colossal earthquake knocked the old place down. It was quite something to see a whole town built in a single style.

Using the airport was a pleasure that airports rarely are because you could drive up to it five minutes before your flight was due to leave, walk in and get on the plane. Actually, that wasn't quite true for me because I needed an extra five minutes to hand over the rental car.

On the flight to Auckland, the girl in the next seat chatted to me about the job interview she had just had. NZers will talk to anyone, and it doesn't matter whether they or the person they are talking to is male or female. I spent a week in Auckland and then flew to Wellington.

Australia is the oldest large inhabited land mass in the world and New Zealand is the youngest. It's still forming. What that means is that there are tremors every day, most so slight you don't notice them, but while I was in South Island we had a biggie—not the worst earthquake NZ had had in twenty years but scary for all that. I had started to think this was a place I could happily live and now I knew it wasn't. I went to the Emirates office and firmed up my flight for the following day.

Dubai was in transition—not the luxury resort drowning in traffic it would become but no longer the fishing village it had been not so long ago. The people were friendly but there was nothing there for me. In any case, that sense that I was getting ready had been hardening. I had a lovely room but I was spending more time in it than I would have liked, partly because it was so hot outside but mostly because I was spending three or four hours a day inside, praying and contemplating. A lot of the contemplation was about the things I had done that I wished I had not done and the people I had hurt who I'd rather not have hurt. The peace I had brought away from the monastery was dissipating. I needed to decide.

I booked a flight to England and another, five days later, back to LA. First class on both legs. Luxury was something I would be giving up soon and I decided to enjoy it one last time. Before I left, I rang my sister. I felt guilty about the little time I had spent with my nephew and niece; what presents could I bring them? I suppose I had in mind some great expensive splash-out that would have their school friends green with envy. Katie said, 'Nothing. Our children are not spoiled and they're not going to be. If you want to give them something, give them a tenner each and tell them to buy books. Ten pounds, Jimmy. No more.'

'I send them more than that each Christmas.'

'Yes, and we wish you wouldn't.'

My mother cried. 'We may never see you again.'

Dad said, 'Look on the bright side, woman. It might have been Katie, deciding to be a nun.'

'Oh, my God! Don't say that! Even as a joke,' she added when we laughed.

I said, 'I'm going to be a lay brother, not a monk. I can write and you can visit. Bennie will be looking after my money. I'll get him to send you the cost of a flight every year. In the front of the plane. And he'll pay for good hotels for you, and car rental. You can drive around, see the country.'

I'd said I was going to be a lay brother, but I didn't have the Master's views on that. What if he thought me an unsuitable recruit? What if he turned me down? When I got home I wrote to him and he wrote back.

Dear Jimmy

I thought we'd be hearing from you again. Yes, we will be happy for you to join us. Come as soon as you are ready— we're always here and the door will open when you knock. Brother James says you were a hard worker and he will be pleased to have you back.

As a lay brother, you will not have to give up whatever assets you have on the outside but please do not spend your time here looking after an estate—you can't talk to God and Mammon at the same time.

I cannot say what the future holds. You will be our first new lay brother for fifteen years; there may never be another. The world has changed and few men now want what we offer. You may outlive the monastery. We must leave what happens to you then to God. And don't forget that you can leave here any time you like.

Go in peace
Master Joseph

I went to see Bennie. Yes, he said, he'd be happy to take over the running of my estate once more. 'A monk, Jimmy? I never would have expected that.'

'Nor me.'

'They say God moves in mysterious ways. Let's hope He knows what He's doing.'

I gave him the instructions about my family and their flights. 'And send them each a hundred dollars at Christmas, and on their birthdays. When Katie's children are eighteen, I want them to have ten thousand dollars each. Another hundred thousand when they marry. But they are not to know that till it happens.'

'Will they live in your house in Venice when they're over here?'

'For as long as they're in LA, yes. You'd better hire a cleaner and a gardener to look after the place.'

'And I'll look in once a month, make sure everything is as it should be.'

I went to one last meeting of the parish men's group and said goodbye to the priest and the church. I sold my car, cut up my credit cards, packed a few clothes and a lot of lined yellow pads and pens into a small bag, got into a taxi and said goodbye to Venice. I didn't know whether I'd ever see it again.

I had four hundred dollars in my pocket when I set off and the taxi fare was only two hundred and fifty. I gave the extra hundred and fifty to the driver. I entered the monastery without a cent.

Chapter 29
Author: James

Iwas a lay brother for ten years. When the first five were up, the Master asked if I wanted to begin my novitiate. I said No. 'I'm not a religious person, ridiculous as that may sound. Not in the way that a monk is. Not as you are. I'm happy to be doing what I am doing and to know that God is here with me.'

'I think that's wise. You led a varied life before you came here. There was a lot of glamour in it. A lot of women. Some men.' His mouth turned down at the corners. 'Do you miss any of that?'

'No. I still wake sometimes dreaming of the things I used to do.'

'How do you handle it?'

'I get up, kneel down and pray till it goes away.'

He nodded. 'Brother James is getting too old to work. A lay brother has never been Gardener but I think you'd be the right choice. Will you do it?'

'I'd be honoured.'

More and more, I was one of those who didn't want to talk when silent time was over. To some extent that was because there were fewer people to talk to—the brothers died, one by one. The conversation I had with the outside workers met my needs for human contact and I spent the rest of my time in prayer and...well. In what? I can't call it contemplation because I didn't contemplate anything. I simply sat in silence and allowed God to take possession of me. Fill me. Whatever you want to call it.

And here's the thing. Something every contemplative religious will understand. I say God took possession of me, but I don't know that. I may simply have been fooling myself. There may have been nothing there at all. I was at peace, and that is all I know. I saw some of the brothers in their later years praying for death to come and I understand why. You don't know. You think you do, but always there is that question. When Christ was dying on the cross he called out, "Why have you forsaken me?" and I don't suppose anyone following him has ever lacked that doubt.

But peace was enough. After all I'd done, peace was enough.

The Master was seventy. That isn't old for some people, but he was coming to the end. Apart from him, there were only three of us left—two monks and me. The rest had all been laid in the small graveyard by the wall. I was fifty-two. The others were all older than the Master. He called me into his study.

'When you came here, I said I didn't know what the future held. We are at the end of our journey. You are the only brother still fit to work.'

'We could hire more outside workers.'

'You mean you could give us another million dollars? Don't say anything, I know it was you. Who else could it have been? We were in need and God sent you to us. No; it is over. I have prayed for guidance and today we received an offer to buy the monastery. They want to turn it into a hotel. Four rooms will be set aside; one of them will be yours. We will be housed and fed without charge until the day we go to the graveyard. I think they see the idea of monks praying in the chapel as a tourist attraction. They will keep you on as gardener until you are too old to work.'

I had known it was coming. I said I would think about it. After three days I returned. 'I will go back into the world.'

'You hardly know it any more.'

'I didn't know it when I came into it as a baby.'

'You had your parents to show you the way.'

'I didn't know it when I first dressed as a girl, or picked up men, or challenged the BBC over a paedophile. I didn't know it when I came to California.' I smiled. Perhaps that's why I made so many mistakes. But now I have something better than parents; I have God.'

'Well. If you're sure. We'll miss you.'

'I'll come back and see you.'

'Don't leave it too long. I have a feeling I may not have much time in that hotel room.'

I never did see the Master again. By the time I was ready, he was gone.

I went to see Bennie and found that my money had been well looked after. I was now worth twenty million dollars. After ten years without any, it felt like a burden.

I moved into my old house in Venice and bought new clothes. I also bought a laptop and began to transfer my stories onto it, typing one finger at a time. That is when I began to write this book.

When I went into a coffee shop for my one a day, or into a restaurant, people smiled at me and often spoke. They remembered who I was. Karen heard I was home and brought her husband and two children to see me. They all looked well. Happy. I felt a "what might have been" sadness, but what's done is done. Then my agent called—the one who found me work. 'You back in business?'

'No-one's going to want an old has-been. Anyway, what about insurance?'

'There's an English TV company looking for someone to guest in a few episodes of a soap. They don't need insurance for that—if you drop dead they'll just put it in the script. You'd be ideal. The money isn't what you used to get.'

'I don't care about money.'

Six weeks later I was in Manchester, shooting the first three episodes. I loved being on set again. It was like I'd never been away.

'The prodigal son,' said my father, grinning from ear to ear. He hugged me. That was something English men had not done when I first went to America. My mother went smiling from neighbour to neighbour, making sure everyone had enough to eat, and Dad kept the glasses topped up. I could see the question in his eyes when I stuck to water.

'I'm not an alcoholic, Dad. I just lost the taste.'

'When you were inside.'

'It wasn't a prison. The opposite, in fact.'

'Well, I'm glad you're out of it.'

Katie was there with her husband, one of their two sons, the son's wife and their toddler, George. (My Dad said, 'How can anyone call a baby George? You can't be a George till you're forty.' But it seemed the name had become fashionable again). The other son was making a life for himself in Australia. The morning after the party, I sat on the sofa with George and we watched *Shaun the Sheep*. Mum praised me for spending time with a child but I thought it was wonderful. In my day we'd only had *Muffin the Mule*.

I was interviewed by several newspapers and I gave them what they wanted. Then the BBC called and asked me to be on a chat show. The host was completely up himself and I didn't take to him. I was the third and last guest. We talked about the movies I'd been in and the people I'd worked with and I went through the routine, saying only nice things when I could have said some shockers. Then he said, 'You used to work for the Beeb. Before you left for better things.'

I took a deep breath. 'Well,' I said, 'it wasn't quite like that. There were things going on here that I didn't like.' His look of false bonhomie was fading. 'Jimmy Savile was a big star at that time. But Savile was a paedophile and the BBC was giving him room and opportunity to ruin young peoples' lives. What's more, they knew it. I challenged that and I was paid off and asked to leave.'

The audience was alive with shocked conversation, but the host was listening to his little earphone. 'Well,' he said, 'that's all we have time for tonight. Tune in next week, folks, and see what fantastic guests we have lined up for you.' He took off his microphone, dropped it on the table and glared at me. 'You've got a fucking nerve.'

* * *

194

I wasn't invited into the Green Room. The show had been recorded and when I watched it the following evening it had been cut just before the host mentioned my time at the Corporation. I had expected to see my remarks about Savile in the press, but no newspaper took it up. When I asked a journalist why not he said, 'Everyone knows about Savile. It's old news.'

'The public don't know.'

'They don't want to, bless them.'

'They don't know because you haven't told them.'

'Jimmy. We also know some stories about a young lady called Lucy. We haven't told the public about those, either. Would you like us to?'

I had been staying at the Savoy while I was in London. Reception called to say there was someone downstairs to see me. It was Helen. I offered her lunch, which we ate in the Grill.

She said, 'The fish is good here. You should bring your father.'

'How's your mother?'

'Dead, I'm afraid. It got her in the end. Dad's gone, too. He gave up when she went. I'm an orphan now.'

'I'm sorry. And you?'

'No, I'm not dead yet.'

'I meant, how are you?'

'Oh, you know. One carries on.'

'Husband? Children?'

'One of each.'

'Happy?'

She stared at me. 'No, James, I'm not happy. I married my husband on the rebound from you and I don't like him.'

'I'm sorry.'

'That's twice you've said you're sorry and I remember telling you twenty years ago after you got yourself fired to stop saying it.' She looked down at her hands. 'What am I doing? I meant this to be a happy reunion. Can we start again?'

I smiled.

'Well, then. My marriage was a mistake but you make your bed and you lie on it. He's a liar and he's mean and he's not as good as you in bed. I've seen all your movies.'

'Oh, dear. Do you want your money back?'

'I enjoyed them. You're a good actor. Well, I suppose I should have known that. I don't watch soaps, ever, but I'm watching this one as long as you're in it. Will you stay in England?'

'Haven't decided yet.'

'If you do, can I be your mistress?'

'You always were frank.'

'Don't call me Frank. And don't answer now; think about it. We had good times together.'

'We did.'

'We could have them again. No ties, just a bit of fun. I've often wished I'd been more forgiving back then.'

'I treated you badly.'

'Yes. You did. We could have got over it. When I told my friends I'd sent you packing they said I was crazy. Ellie said you and I were perfect for each other. She was right. And the last thing I said to you. It was pretty horrible.'

'Yes. Yes, it was.'

'Oh, God, you remember.'

'I deserved it.'

'No-one deserves to be spoken to like that. The only excuse is that I was overwhelmed by grief. I'd been so sure you were the one. Then worrying about my mother, and coming back to work to hear those things. Listen, this stuff about a monastery: is it true?'

'I was a lay brother, not a monk. But, yes, it's true.'

'Why?'

'Oh.' I spread my hands on the table and she picked one up and kissed it. 'Looking back...I thought I was happy, but I wasn't. Then I had a heart attack and while I was floating around between life and heaven's gates I saw God. I wanted to see Him again. It had been a moment of absolute peace and I hadn't had any of that.'

'Do you think you really did? See God, I mean?'

'I have no idea. Really. But the monastery brought me what I longed for more than anything. I don't know for sure whether God exists or not, even though I feel him with me all the time, and to be perfectly truthful I don't know if He ever looks at us even if He's there, but I found a way to live in peace and I'd have given anything for that.'

'You never showed any sign of this when we were together.'

'I was a child. A naïf, overgrown schoolboy. People should have slapped me down and told me to grow up. I shudder when I think of some of the things I did.'

'The knickers?'

'The knickers. What did I think I was doing? I'm a man, not a woman. Knickers belong on someone with the bum to fill them.' I closed my two hands around one of hers. 'Someone like you.'

'So you'll think about it?'

'I'll think about it. What are you doing this afternoon?'

'I must get back to work. And this evening we have to go to my mother-in-law's birthday do. I'd never be forgiven if I missed that.'

'I'm checking out in the morning. We're filming in Manchester.'

We exchanged phone numbers, and Helen left. The temptation had been there and I'm not sure I'd have resisted if she'd been able to go to my room with me right then, but when she'd gone and I could look at it straight I knew I wasn't going to be part of an adulterous relationship. That was something I'd never done, surprising as that may be.

Chapter 30
Author: James

I was tempted to stay in England but the temptation waned. The place had changed since I'd lived there. When I walked through Manchester in the evening, there were youths shouting and girls throwing up and fighting, clawing at each other on the ground with their skirts rucked up and their knickers showing. I don't mean the place was full of them because it wasn't, but there were enough.

And there was a rudeness, a self-regarding contempt for others that was new.

It wasn't like that in Venice Beach. There people still had the civilised respect for other people that I'd grown up with. I mentioned that to someone and he blamed immigration. 'There's lots of studies to show that society breaks down when you introduce too many people from other cultures. Look what's happened in Sweden. And look at Japan—they make it hard to immigrate and their society has weathered all sorts of storms.'

'Maybe. But America was built by immigrants and you don't see this breakdown there.'

I wasn't going to maintain any sense of peace if I stayed. I was turned down a further twenty soap episodes. I did a cameo on a children's TV programme and was offered cocaine in the Green Room. Of course, I'd seen that before, but not on a children's show. I couldn't imagine Captain Kangaroo offering anyone a hit.

I booked a flight to LA, said goodbye to Mum, Dad and Katie and went home.

My agent was delighted by the reports of my appearances in England. 'The offers are flooding in. You can take your pick.'

'I'll say it again: what about insurance?'

'No longer an issue. You've been working, there wasn't a problem, the heart attack was more than ten years ago and you've been fine since then. We can get cover.'

We went through the scripts and I picked out three that

were worth a close look. The parts on offer were not quite what I had once had, but that happens anyway as you get older. No-one was going to see me now as a credible contender for the young maiden's hand. What I was looking at was elder statesman roles, a foil to the upcoming star. The young hero's boss; the teacher; the father. I picked that one first—I'd never had a child of my own and I relished the opportunity to play a part I'd missed out on in life.

Then came the big one. It was an unexpected joy to land the breakout part so late in my career.

A ten part TV series (in the end it ran for six years and there were a hundred and twenty episodes) set in a big city police department. Two cops just starting out, one black and female and the other male and Hispanic, are tutored in their work by the experienced sergeant who has seen it all but never become bitter or disillusioned. They fight against him—what can this old honky teach smart dudes like them?—but over the course of the first series they come to see his wisdom and they learn from him. It was built around me; in every episode I drew on some incident from the distant past to see the way forward but I always made sure they got the credit. Over the course of six years the writers built me a back story—the wife shot dead by the vengeful father of a boy I'd sent to the gas chamber; the son from whom I had been estranged but with whom I was reconciled (it took a whole series to complete that reconciliation); the parents who, as I discovered in the third series, had adopted me after my parents died in a shootout with police; the woman who had carried a torch for me since before I was married but knew I would never take up her offers because I still grieved for my dead love. Corny? I should just say so, but the viewers lapped it up. Angie Dickinson made a guest appearance as the cop from another city helping to catch one of her own serial killers; Bob Denver of all people played a hostile defence attorney in two episodes; Tony Curtis played a cameo as an artist (the pictures in his studio were his own). We had other names—people were clamouring to be part of our success. The ratings monstered.

Over the life of the programme we had to replace each of

the smart young dudes three times because they had made their names working with me and gone on to big-screen roles of their own. While we were negotiating a seventh series I came out of the barber shop after a haircut, looked both ways and started across the road when two men came running out of a liquor store followed by the Korean owner carrying a shot gun. He raised it to his waist and fired. He missed both men. He hit me. The spread of pellets caught my back, my neck and my throat. My larynx was wrecked.

The hospital doctors were wonderful. When I came out of intensive care they told me they could rebuild the shattered voice box and I would speak again. Not right away and not with the same quality of voice, but I'd speak. They were right. It took six years, but they did it and when I was sixty-six I was again ordering dinner and talking to neighbours without having to write everything down on a pad I carried with me. From sixty to sixty-six, though, I'd been dumb and there's very little call for TV actors who can't speak.

Those six years put my sense of peace and my faith in God's care to a severe test. The priest at the church I attended had changed during my time in the monastery but the new one was a good man. He didn't speak to me in platitudes and I was grateful for that. Nevertheless, I could feel my faith waning.

I booked into the Monastery Hotel. I didn't tell them that I knew the place, but of course they had my name. The manager came to meet me when I checked in. 'Mister Carlton, it is an honour to have you here again. You will find the place much changed, and for the better, I hope.'

'Thank you. Look, I just want to spend a quiet week here. No fuss.'

'Of course. But you will eat dinner in the dining room? We still call it the refectory. The other guests will recognise you.'

'That's all right.' I knew how to handle fans, however

intrusive. 'But all I'm looking for is rest and peace.'

'Yes, sir. I will instruct the staff that you are to be protected as much as possible.'

'Are any of the brothers still here?'

He spread out his arms. Watching him was like seeing a mime artist conveying thoughts without words. 'Alas, the last one died a month ago. He is buried in the graveyard with the others.'

'I hope you will keep a plot there for one last guest.'

The arms rose in the air like a bookie's tictac man. 'That will be such an honour.' And something else to sell his hotel, but he was welcome to that. 'We have set aside your old room for you.'

It looked nothing like it had when I had been here before, but a sense of calm settled on me when I entered. I tipped the porter and told him I needed nothing. When he had gone, I knelt on the floor, spread my arms across the bed and emptied my mind. He would come, or He would not.

Two hours later, I walked in the garden. One of the men I had trained hugged me. 'Welcome back, Brother Jimmy.'

'They treat you well?'

'I have no complaints.'

Then I sat in the graveyard. The bench Brother Timothy had built so lovingly was still there; the gardeners tended the graves and kept them free of weeds; there were gravel paths between them that had not been there before. The earth on the latest grave was fresh, but beginning to blend with the others. I sat on Brother Timothy's bench and looked at the Master's grave. I prayed. I opened my heart, and something entered into it. It was as though my body were settling, just as the graves had done one by one.

The gardener tapped me on the shoulder. 'It's growing dark, Brother Jimmy.'

I shook myself. 'Shouldn't you have gone home? How long have I been sitting here?'

'I've been watching over you. Keeping guests away.'

'Thank you.' When I stood up I was stiff and I walked back to my room like an old man. I rang Room Service. 'I'd like to eat in my room this evening.'

'Yes, Mister Carlton. What would you like? We have soup, salad from the garden, some really nice lamb, a roast of beef.'

'Just bread and cheese, please. A piece of fruit if you have it. A glass of water.'

'Wine? Coffee?'

'No. Just the bread and cheese and the fruit and a glass of water.'

'Well, sir, if you're sure that's all.' I had disappointed him.

I had lived in this place for ten years without once going outside the walls. I didn't go out now. The manager talked to me about souvenir shops and cafes in the European style and a civic walk, but everything I wanted was here.

I made an arrangement with the maid that she would wait till midday to clean my room. Each morning I rose at five and knelt to pray. At seven I went to the refectory where I smiled at the other guests, talked to those who would not settle for less, and took breakfast. There was no oatmeal but they did have boiled eggs. The bakery had closed and the bread was not as good as it had been in my day. I drank my single cup of coffee, waving away offers of top-ups.

Then I went back to my room and prayed again.

I examined my faith, but the fact was that I didn't know. I was a believer, but I didn't know. I knew there was a God because I talked to him and he talked to me, but I didn't know. It was the dilemma that all believers face: you believe, but you can't know. What is demanded of you is faith without proof. Did Christ really rise from the dead? It sounds unlikely, but we are faced with the cowardice of the disciples before the stone was rolled away and their bravery afterwards. Would they have acted that way if they had not seen, alive, a man they knew to have died? I certainly wouldn't have.

In the afternoons I walked in the garden, enjoyed the sun and the open air and talked to the gardeners. Then back into my room, where I read my stories again and started to write this book. I was a faster typist now but it was still slow going and I had a sense that time was not on my side. In the evenings I ate in my room and then I went to bed and slept in peace like a baby.

When I went home, I felt a heaviness that might have been spiritual but that I knew was physical. I went to the doctor and when I went back a week later he did not try to mislead me. 'All the test results are in. If we had found this a year ago, we might have been able to do something. As it is...'

'How long have I got?'

'A month? Six weeks?'

I thought of this book unfinished on my laptop and the work still to do.

He said, 'When the end comes, there is a good place...a nursing home...'

'A hospice, you mean? A place to die with dignity?'

'That's all you can hope for now, Jimmy.'

'Give me their phone number.'

I worked on the book every minute I could. I cannot say "tirelessly" because I tire more quickly with each day that passes, but now I have reached this point and that will have to suffice. I go to the hospice tomorrow. I have spoken to Katie and sent her an airline ticket; when she comes I will give her this laptop and leave it to her to decide what to do with it. If you read my book, if you have got this far, you see me warts and all. The young man I was, the girl I pretended to be, the men I gave myself to, the women I loved and who loved me and the way I treated them. I hope Margaret is okay. I hope our little girl found a loving home and is living a happy life. God, please take care of her. I hope...

I am done with hoping. Lord God, if you are there and if you are listening to me, I am sorry for my sins. Forgive me. Lord, in your mercy, hear my prayer.

There is nothing else.

Chapter 31
Author: James's sister

If you think I should not have published this book, I am sorry. I thought Jimmy deserved to have his story known and there it is.

I arrived two days after Jimmy wrote the last sentence of Chapter 30 and stayed with him for all the time he had left. The nursing home that he calls a hospice gave me a bed and I ate in the cafeteria. He died that second evening, oblivious to me and speaking to the God he believed loved him and to whom he could offer his soul in confidence.

I hope he was right. God, if you hear, please take care of my little brother.

END

18507802R00115

Printed in Great Britain
by Amazon